Five Spirits in the Room

Five Spirits in the Room

A novel by

Rebecca Conaty Bruce

Lineage Independent Publishing
Marriottsville, MD

ISBN (paperback): 9781958418031

First published in the United States of America

Publisher: Lineage Independent Publishing,

Marriottsville, MD, USA

Maryland Sales and Use Tax Entity: Lineage Independent Publishing,

Marriottsville, MD 21104

www.lineage-indypub.com

lineagepublishing@gmail.com

I have several dear friends, former classmates, and acquaintances that have experienced great loss. No one dreams about outliving their children. I want you to know that my heart goes out to you Nancy, Cheryl, Linda, Kathy, Melanie, Carol and many others that have touched my life in some way. As well as those who have experienced a tragic loss in a school shooting attacking our children. This should never happen. If only there was truly a secret good-bye club.

I send you much love…

Think of grief as a maze made of hedges and being lost in it is more than okay.

Table of Contents

Foreword

No parent or grandparent should ever outlive their progeny, regardless of the circumstances. The grief and sense of loss is pervasive and paralytic. I know because my wife and I are members of the group… We lost our adult son to cancer twelve years ago.

Rebecca Conaty Bruce's story captures the essence of what could happen on either side of the boundary between life and death.

From the living: "We are always encouraged to move on and try to get back to normal. "Move on from the denial, accept the facts and get on with your life. However, our normal is changed forever… Our life didn't end the day our child died even though it feels that way and some hoped it would. We are still entitled to a future, good or bad."

From the deceased: "Love, we leave love behind. That is what Life After Death means. You give so much of yourself to the people you love while you are alive that so much remains behind. What survives is not our body, but love. Love survives."

Reading Rebecca's words have had a cathartic effect. Sure, it's just another day, but it is the day that our world changed forever. We'd like to bring our son back… we'd like to have had just one more day… we'd like for him to still be here in body. We *know* he is here in spirit, in our memories, and no one can take that away.

Michael Paul Hurd
Author/Publisher
Lineage Independent Publishing

1~The Group of the Secret Good-byes Club

"What is happening? Where am I? Why am I here?"

In the corner was a small thin boy, delicate in structure, struggling to stand as if he just woke up from a very long sleep. His eyes grew wide behind his thick black glasses as he became aware of his surroundings. Brushing his hand over his crew cut, he stared into the room with disbelief and wonder.

A second boy appeared by the coffee service with the same expression as the first boy. In the back of the room behind the rows of stacked rusty metal chairs a third figure appeared. Popping up like flowers blooming in a field, a fourth male figure stepped out of the shadows to look around glancing at the others who seemed to appear out of nowhere, just like he did. A red-haired curvy girl about age nineteen appeared from the shadows in the corner and placed her hands on her hips. "Where am I? I don't understand what is happening…"

Soon there were five all together. They looked at each other with surprise on their curiously pale faces. "I don't know," the small boy replied. "it is like I was asleep, then I was here…in this old building. It's definitely stuck in the 70's by the décor. Where is this exactly?"

Examining their clothes and touching their faces with disbelief, they looked around the room with questioning gaze. Evident in their startled expressions, their sudden appearances in this room were unexpected, unplanned. Questions were swirling in their minds, *"Why they were here, in this building, at this place and this time?"*

A slight fog was slowly rolling in as summer was fading, hinting that fall was just around the corner. The weather turned cool at night and the smell of autumn bonfires left a hint in the air. A new group meeting was about to begin at the East Bay Community Center. The center had been a place for weddings and birthday celebrations in the past, now it was used mostly for support groups.

A once well-kept field outside the center for community football teams and soccer fields full of children now was a forgotten wildflower meadow with cookie cutter houses just beyond the reach of the meadow. Inside the center, the walls were darkly paneled with tile floors showing its age. Stacks of folding chairs and tables leaned against the outside walls. The orange paisley curtains covered old crank windows reminiscent of the era the center was built.

Various groups met there different nights of the week. Alcoholics Anonymous met every Thursday followed by a yoga group on Friday. Wednesday was the night set aside for parents who have lost a son or daughter suddenly or unexpectedly. "Angel parents" they are creditably called, whether it was by accidental death, illness, or suicide, a young child, or adult child. A parent losing a child is suddenly thrust into a swirling cyclone, continually circling around them with items and memories of their child. Instead of flying cows and trees, they simply stand and stare as the wind blows bits and pieces of their life in front of their eyes. Some have described it as being lost in a foggy pain and grief filled maze they cannot find their way out of, and that is okay.

It was a new start up group, recently formed with a new director that had himself lost a child unexpectedly. James Arnold and his wife, Sarah, had tried several avenues to deal with their grief after losing their eight-year-old son. Navigating through grief and several support groups, James knew with vivid clarity that he needed to start this group for others who suffered from the misconception that the pain will never end.

Sarah did not cope well. Depression set in so deep she was not able to speak her son's name. It deepened until one day James came home from work and found her in a catatonic state. James still continued to seek help wherever he could. While dealing with his grief with the help of a professional counselor, James became curiously aware that he felt more comfortable around other parents who had suffered a similar loss than those who had lost a parent or loving auntie.

James needed a connection. Other parents who had lost a child seemed to understand what he was going through much better than the neighbor who brought a casserole or his former boss who just avoided him. So, after an unexpected occurrence, James planned with the proper agencies to form the group he now calls the "Secret Good-byes Club" A special group for Angel Parents. It was different from all other help groups with a special twist at the end: a miracle that no one dared to talk about when the five weeks were over.

Five Spirits

Those who attended the group meetings left with incredible secret experiences, making them hold the miraculous ending close to their heart for fear the peaceful feelings would disappear. Hospitals, social workers, and churches referred and encouraged the parents to join a group when they lose a child suddenly. Not all groups are the same, this one was special, different, and unique. Word spread that a new group with positive results had been formed and James was flooded with inquiries. James carefully chose which parents got to attend then formally notified them in the mail with a golden ticket in a crisp white envelope.

You have been invited to attend the Five
Week Session of the Secret Good-bye Club.

It was always the same: one or both parents did not want to grieve publicly in a group to talk about their feelings. This group was formed for last-chance parents unable to grasp reality and the grieving taking over their lives. If parents preferred to stay shut up and grieve alone they never moved forward.

Alone is never a good thing. James knew this because of what happened to his own wife. Sarah refused to go to meetings denying to the core that their son was gone. James floundered looking for ways to live on by himself.

Most of the sessions James held had a high percentage of single parents. No one ever left unsatisfied; he made sure of it.

2~Day One

Tonight was the first night of another five-week session for the good-bye club. James was expecting five sets of parents who had all lost a child. Small towns like these can post a sign for a church picnic and have a grand turnout – but post a sign for grieving parents to gather and no one wants to be seen coming in the door. James did not advertise; he just reserved the community center for Wednesdays. All attendees were personally chosen.

Grief is a strong, sometimes overwhelming emotion and James knew this first-hand. It is the strongest of all the emotions we experience in a lifetime. Usually, the soul knows how to heal the mind; it is the mind that does not cooperate.

Arriving a few minutes early to brew the coffee, James switched on the halogen lights still hanging from the yellowed ceiling. Coffee always made people feel at ease and made the room smell just right. He then carefully laid out a spread of various cheeses, crackers, and chips on a blue tablecloth. Donuts were usually the snack of choice at meetings, but James had it all planned out. There would be a different theme and different refreshment at every meeting. All with a special purpose and chosen to inspire memories of the lives lost. James then began arranging the metal chairs in a circle leaving space between them. James left an empty chair between each parent placing a box of tissues on the chair to allow space.

Five Spirits

As adults started shuffling in, it was obvious they were hesitant and guarded. They nodded at James, darting their eyes around the room, then pulling at their clothes nervously. Taking seats with plenty of space between them gave a sense that they were not crowded nor forced to be here. The first woman entered alone and took a seat glancing sideways around the room as she pushed the hair out of her face. She slumped in her chair biting her lip as she clutched her purse tightly in her lap.

"That's my mom!" the young boy shouted from the back of the room. *"Hey mom, can you see me? I'm over here!"* he said, waving his arms. He was the second boy to appear. He had dark curly hair and large brown eyes and was the most animated of the group. He had a hard time standing still, always shifting his weight from one foot to the other. The woman he called Mom clutched her purse in her lap as if it was her shield of protection. She pulled out a tissue and held it to her nose, hiding half her face but still peeking around with one eye, hoping to go unnoticed. Her name was Melanie Thomas and she had lost her son, Harry. She wore a comfortable flowered maxi dress and sensible shoes. Her hair was pulled back in a tight ponytail that causied her ears to protrude slightly.

Moving into the light to join the others was the taller male. He stood towering over the others. Confused, he stood beside young Harry. "I don't think they can hear us, little dude. Those are my parents over there." *"Hey, Dad! Look over here!"* he said. He had long blonde hair, tight black jeans with army boots that he laced up tightly. "See, they can't hear us or see us. I've been standing over there in the shadow for a while now."

Harry looked up at the new guy and tugged on his shirt. "Hey what is your name? I'm Harry."

"Aaron. Why am I here?" he asked.

"I don't know," said Harry, shrugging his shoulders.

Next there was Derek scowling behind his hoodie, making it four males and one female to appear. Ranging in heights, Aaron was able to stand behind the other four and watch as his parents took a seat in the circle, never acknowledging him. He stared down at his army boots wondering what he did wrong.

As the last few adults entered the room James invited everyone to help themselves to grab a cup of coffee and a snack before taking a chair. "The meeting will begin in a few minutes, so if you would like to take your coffee back to your seat, it is fine. This old carpet has seen better days so there are no restrictions as to food and drink."

Being the first meeting, only a few were comfortable enough to help themselves to a cup of coffee and James knew this would change as time went by and resistance to being in a group subsided. A few wandered around looking at the pictures on the walls and snacked on cheese and crackers. James held hope that he could help these parents navigate their grief and help them move to a feeling of peace. He was determined to change their lives by changing the way they control their grief. He also offered answers to difficult questions all parents have.

Derek, the most athletic of the bunch stepped forward as the group of five watched in awe wondering what was happening. "I guess for whatever this meeting is about, my mother came with her new boyfriend," he said pointing at a nicely dressed man. "I am not even going to look at him." Shoving his hands into the pockets of his denim jeans, he lowered his head. He kicked his shoes together, his chestnut hair falling in his eyes. "There were many reasons I stopped dancing in the rain, and he was one of the reasons," said Derek. "I guess I didn't handle things well at all, I messed up."

James waited to see if anymore were coming and everyone had a chance to get coffee before he closed the door and began. He stood in front of the group and announced that it was time to get started. Everyone quietly took their seat. James was usually slightly nervous and calmly excited to start the group because he knew in the end every parent would be changed forever. James straightened his back and addressed the group for the first time.

"My name is James Arnold. I will be your host. You have all been handpicked for this five-week class and filled out the proper forms for admission. We can all keep it to informal introductions. We are all here because we have suffered loss and for some reason we are still suffering, not having reached acceptance – the final stage of grief. Thank you for being brave enough to come tonight. We will meet for five weeks every Wednesday night. It is *more* important that you attend the meeting than if you *share* your story. However, sharing your story is very beneficial. This is much more than just grief counseling. It will be a path to heartfelt peace. Every good-bye is special; this group is the special good-bye club"

The nicely dressed man rolled his eyes and looked at his watch. James noticed his actions but looked the other way. He understood that it was hard to even show up tonight. It was similar to what he himself had also felt when attending meetings. If they had their choice, these parents would most likely still be curled up on a couch in the dark. "In the end, all will be revealed and understood," James thought to himself.

As James began to tell his personal story of grief, the only girl in the group of five came forward from the shadows to stand beside the other four. Looking bewildered she stood staring. "What is going on and why are we in this room?" she muttered. "We can see them, but they cannot see us at all? Is this some sort of magic?"

"Hey who are you? Were you here all the time?" asked Harry. "I mean, what is your name?"

"I'm Darcy. Yes, I was hiding over there because I'm confused. I shouldn't be here. I don't know what is happening"

"We are all confused. Are your parents here too?" asked Aaron, joining in the conversation.

"My dad is over there" she pointed. I guess my mom couldn't come. That is him over there with the red hair just like mine. He always told me it was the luck of the Irish to have red hair. And before any of you ask, it did not bring me any luck" chuckled Darcy.

Swiveling his head to look at the other four, Harry spoke up. "Hey, has anyone figured out why we are here and why our parents can't see us yet? I mean, this is weird, right?" asked Harry.

As the four of them stood looking around the room at their parents with sad looks on their faces a fifth person stepped out from the shadows to join them.

"Who are you? Did you just get here? asked Harry.

"I am Pattimore. Nah, I have been watching. Looks like a meeting of some sort with all our parents. Feels like parent-teacher conference night." Pausing, he noticed the other four staring at him. "I am naturally short if you were all wondering. I have heard all the jokes, so don't bother. He is a Shorty shortcake, Mr. no legs or my favorite of all time…Is the weather better down there where you are?" he smirked. Pattimore had gotten so used to being made fun of he had added his own snarky comments trying to beat them to the punch. Looking up to the others in the group pausing for a reaction, he then looked back straight ahead resting his head in his hands. "Stop staring! It is not polite or I will bite your kneecaps" he added.

Leaning down to look Pattimore in the eyes, Darcy, the only female in the odd group, smiled. "Sorry… I didn't mean to stare. Love your bowtie by the way. Do you know what is going on?" asked Darcy. "We are all confused"

"No, but wow! That is my mom over there in the black pants and pointy shoes. But she can't see me. None of them can see us." "*I am right here mom!*" he waved making a point. "She is the one crying. She cries all the time" he said.

Pattimore was the smallest of the five strangers with small childlike legs and big teeth. He was a younger boy, about eleven, sporting a crew cut, a plaid shirt and a bow tie that he nervously tugged on quite often. "Let me show you all something," he said. "In case you have any doubts about why they cannot see us… " Pattimore then strutted past the others in his usual swagger and over to a woman he had called Mom. The woman wore glasses similar to his, teased hair and a thread bare dress. The other four watched as he bravely without concern at all, walked around her and waved his hands in front of the woman's face.

"What are you doing? Are you crazy?" shouted Harry. "Come back before she sees you"

"That is totally bonkers, little dude, if you ask me" said Derek.

Aaron took a step forward motioning for Pattimore. "We are unsure of what is happening. I wouldn't play around like that little guy. That lady has that puckered mouth like she could slap the tar out of someone!" chimed in Aaron.

Pattimore put his hands on his hips, looking disappointed at the comments from the group. He straightened his bow tie and placing one arm in front and the other arm wrapped in the back, he gave a strange little bow toward the others like an actor at the end of a play.

"Watch and learn, people!" Pattimore shouted again at the others. Pattimore stood waving one hand toward the others to get their attention then pointing at the woman in the chair as he dramatically thrust one foot forward like a swordsman. "This is my mother here," Pattimore shouted. "She does not see me. She is staring right through me as if I was a pane of window glass. I can dance, wave, or even make a fart noise with my mouth, which I was never allowed to do at home. She will still not hear me or see me"

"Bow tie dude is a little kooky," whispered Harry.

"I think he is brave. My mother would have sent me to my room if I got up in her face like that," said Darcy the only girl in the group.

Pattimore began buzzing around in front of the woman, flapping his arms like an annoying fly at a picnic. Stopping he lowered his head briefly then in his usual fashion he popped back up saying *"Boo!"* The woman never flinched. He turned toward the others laughing. "It is okay. Do you get it now, or do I have to spell it out for you guys?"

Derek stepped back and folding his arms across his chest. "No need to spell it out, little dude, you are a bucket of chuckles. I am just waiting for the show. Your momma is going to get real mad" Pattimore stopped and put his hands up in the air with a look of disbelief. "Haven't you all figured it out yet?" he shouted. They cannot hear us, see us, or talk to us because we are all DEAD!"

3~Sharing

James began pacing around the circle of chairs as he spoke. Attempting to break the ice, he started each meeting with a story that the parents could relate to, then sat in the circle as part of the group while they began to open up and share. Some of the parents watched as though they were curious to hear what James had to say and some kept their eyes lowered. It was so quiet you could hear a pin drop as James told them the story of his own personal loss.

He told this story many times in his groups but felt it necessary to let them know he had also been through something similar to what they are experiencing in their early grief stage. Each time he told his story he felt the sting. Grief never goes away; it just takes on different forms. James looked around the room as he slowly made his way to the middle of the circle making eye contact with each one, and then cleared his throat.

"It was a cold day with thick marshmallow clouds. A sign that let us know it was going to be a heavy coat and mittens type of day. Temperatures dropped rapidly from in the fifties to the low thirties in a matter of hours then quickly plummeted to below freezing." James sighed, then continued on. "My son dressed himself that day for school. We were not there to see him off. See, my wife and I both worked at jobs away from home. Sarah, my wife was always rushing to get our son off to school before she left for work. I had already left the house heading to my big important corporate job, so it all fell on her. My son, Joshua, missed his bus that day, so he decided to just walk to school. He didn't ask permission; he just decided not to bother us. He never missed the bus before and was certainly never allowed to walk."

James paused to look around the room, nowing that listening to others tell their story would bring up emotions we were all trying hard to suppress. It is a normal response to feel uncomfortable. When Joshua died, it was as though James had been stabbed in the gut over and over and over again. A tormented, physical pain, very hard to describe. In fact, even though the pain only eases a bit, parents want to be able to talk about their children. They have to. They need to.

They wanted to hear stories of how their child loved to play sports or win at the science fair. It is called keeping their memory alive. If friends, family and even those just trying to help would realize we wanted to talk about it down to the jumping in the puddle details even if it is uncomfortable for other people.

James swallowed hard before he continued. He looked down at the floor for a moment reaching for courage. He felt that emotional sting every time he shared his story. Choking back emotions, he brought his head up to meet the other parents straight on. If he can be brave, then maybe they can also.

"It was an accident" James continued. "We failed as parents to keep a watchful eye on our little boy, but in the end it was just an accident. A sudden unplanned death by accident. Our son, Joshua, was found frozen in a puddle only three feet deep on the side of a busy road. He forgot his coat and mittens and was only wearing his favorite cotton shirt. He was smart not to walk in the road but must have fallen in the ditch not knowing it was deep and full of water under the thin ice. Boys can't pass by a puddle without wanting to splash," he chuckled. "With the freezing temperatures, his heart failed from shock. We were told it was quick and not a lot of pain – as if that made it easier… It didn't, by the way."

Pattimore's mother, the woman in the black pants and pointy shoes, let out a loud gasp. As others in the room looked over at her, she hid her face and stood up as though she was ready to run. James stood in front of her, taking care to not approach too close nor reach out, knowing some people do not want to be touched. When grief hits due to a death of a loved one, everyone wants to hug you and cry with you. Sometimes you prefer not to be slobbered all over.

"Mrs. Gilliam, is it?" asked James. "From the paperwork you filled out, I see you lost your son, Pattimore. Is that right?"

"Yes, and you can call me Ruth. I am sorry, but I think I should leave now," she muttered.

"If you must leave, then by all means the door is open. But Ruth, I would love it if you stayed. I need to talk about my son, and I bet you do too," said James folding his hands. "Please stay, Ruth"

Ruth nodded dabbing her eyes and took her seat reluctantly. Causing a scene is something she wanted to avoid at all costs. James continued to walk around the room and stopped in the middle of the circle. "Everyone in this room has lost a child. We have all been blindsided with misery. Sitting here is the mother of Pattimore Gilliam, over there is the mother of Derek Tenner, and then we have parents of Darcy, Aaron, and young Harry's mother seated here. Five parents of five children who died. We all have death in common even though it is a club we never wanted to join."

James again took a deep breath and allowed a long pause before he continued speaking. Crying was always the first meeting expectancy, so he allowed time for the sniffling and nose-blowing.

"You all have heard of the five stages of grief starting with denial. I also gripped hard at that first stage. I told the police it wasn't my son, not Joshua, they must have made a mistake. Of course, it quickly went straight to anger, the second stage, when I arrived at the hospital to identify the body. I was so angry I wanted to hit someone, hurt someone, or even hurt myself. I blamed everyone…" he paused.

"Remember, grief is powerful. So powerful it can control you if you allow it. I blamed my wife, she lashed back at me, and we were a mess. That is grief and it is normal to feel that way. Don't ever judge someone by the way they grieve. We all handle the five stages differently."

As James paused, Pattimore took a seat on the floor and put his head into his hands. "See I told you my mom always cries," he muttered. "I would bring home a note from the teacher and she would cry, I made honor roll and she would cry, science award…tears by the bucket full."

"You should cut your mom some slack if we are really dead like you say. I suppose our parents should be acting sad," commented Harry, taking a seat next to Pattimore. "If they don't cry, what would that mean? Look at my mom. She just stares off into space. From a helicopter mom to a soft puddle, that woman. She used to laugh all the time," said Harry. "Now staring at the floor has become her passion."

Soon Darcy flopped on the floor next to the two boys and propped her elbows on her knees. "Dang! We must be dead; I mean I know I am dead. I remember everything. I was just scared and hoping it wasn't true," remarked Darcy. "That's why I'm so confused. If I am dead, why am I here?"

"Are you saying you remember how you died, Darcy?" asked Pattimore. "For some reason, I don't remember anything."

"What do you mean?" asked Darcy.

"I lived a sandcastle life. Built it up, added a nice bowtie, ready to display my genius and wham! One wave came in and knocked my life away" explained Pattimore. "I think I know why but I am not really sure. I don't remember feeling any pain. Shouldn't there have been pain?"

Darcy pushed her hair behind her ears and scooted near Pattimore. "That is a very sad analogy of your short life Pattimore. There will never be another you, Pattimore. Someone may be taller or prettier but never just like you. Myself, I remember being in a car accident. I was busy applying my lip gloss, singing to the radio. When I looked up, the dump truck in front of me stopped suddenly. I felt pain for a short moment I think, then peace like I was floating," commented Darcy. "Floating like a feather from a bird… do you know that feeling?"

Derek joined the other three on the floor. "I remember feeling peaceful also, Darcy," said Derek. "A strange feeling of letting go came over me like a fog. What do you think that means?"

Aaron stood facing the others seated on the floor. "Pattimore is right: we must be dead. I know I died, but why I am here in this room is the question. Are we stuck?" asked Aaron peeking out from his hood. "Is this some kind of an alternate universe or something?"

Pattimore strained to look up at the tall boy named Aaron. "Let's all sit down and think about this. It is straining my neck looking up at you. Man, you are way too tall, Aaron!" replied Pattimore.

Aaron smiled and then sat down with the other four and shoved his hands in the pockets of his hoodie. "It all feels strangely normal."

Derek leaned forward folding his hands in his lap. "Isn't there a heaven we should go to? My mother always talked about God and heaven," asked Derek.

"Does this old building look like heaven to you, Derek?" snarled Pattimore. "I am not sure Heaven has paneling on the walls."

"Maybe we are not good enough to go, so this is a short stopover. I mean, I did a few bad things I suppose, but I did not mean to do those things," Derek stated.

"None of us understand anything right now except that we all died and suddenly we are here in this old community center. Let's just listen to this James talk so we can figure it out," said Aaron.

"Shhh... you guys. I think my dad is about to talk and I can't wait to hear this," said Darcy getting up off the floor to listen.

James paused for everyone to digest what he had just shared with the group about his son. He then walked over and took a seat in the circle trying to give the impression he was one of them, a parent still navigating grief just like all the parents in the room. He opened up the floor asking if anyone felt up to sharing their story. Mr. Williams, Darcy's father, stood up and pulled his coat tighter.

James acknowledged him. "Mr. Williams, if you feel more comfortable sitting, it is your choice. We do not have any strict guidelines in this group except to speak as though your child can hear you. Please feel free to share whatever is on your mind"

"I am Dave, the father of Darcy. My wife Nanette couldn't be here tonight because of work. Darcy was my only daughter. She was a daddy's girl and we shared such a great bond. We both loved fishing and food. Her death was also an accident, but it didn't matter, it still hit me hard. When I got to the anger stage, I even blamed Darcy. I blamed her boyfriend, her mother, even her education came into question. How can a smart lovely girl be so careless?" he paused to wipe his eyes. "We raised her better. She was beautiful and looked a lot like me. Now we are suffering. All I want to do is go fishing. It helps me deal with the loss. She was my fishing buddy, and it keeps me away from people. I cannot handle all the people. I agreed to come to this group reluctantly as a final try to find some meaning and perhaps some peace." He finished and took his seat.

"Mr. Williams, I can certainly understand your pain and your grief. Only a parent who has lost a child can truly understand another parent's pain. In your grief, it is normal to blame others. Blaming is a part of the process; do not feel guilty about blaming the person who died or anyone else. This is the place to let it all out," said James. "We all do it and it is normal"

Mr. Williams nodded in agreement then sniffled trying to hold back the tears. His face grimaced as he sat back folding his arms.

James had gotten used to the long silent pauses and knew it was necessary if the group was going to succeed. It takes time and he was going to give the parents plenty of it.

"We are only going to discuss the first two stages tonight. I want to hear about your denial and your anger as well. The anger everyone tells you to hold in and just deal with it. I also want to hear about the blame and the joy, and then the happy times. I want to hear all the positive things about the child you lost, were they tall, did they love dinosaurs or football. I want you to speak about them as though they were in this very room. Would anyone else want to share now?" asked James.

Slowly James looked around the room. He just needed a sign that a parent wanted to speak but was holding back. "Does anyone have a story of denial, anger, or blaming they want to share and get off their chest?" he paused. "The purpose of this group is being with other parents who have been through the same emotions, so they understand your feelings because they have experienced the same or similar"

"You can speak without judgment here?" mumbled Mrs. Gilliam as she looked up. "I would like to speak; I mean talk about my Pattimore. If that is okay?"

"Oh, this should be interesting," said Pattimore, straightening his bow tie. "Watch out for the waterworks, everyone!"

"My Pattimore is…umm… was a very smart little boy. Most mothers think their child is smart, but Pattimore was a child genius," she said looking at her folded hands in her lap. "I never graduated from high school, so I don't know where he got his brains from"

"Wow, I didn't know that about my mom," whispered Pattimore. "She never told me that. It explains why she never read my papers"

"I don't think we know a lot about our parents," commented Darcy as she anxiously stepped forward, twisting her hair. "I am going to sit next to my dad; I never knew how much he enjoyed fishing with me"

"Go wherever you want just be quiet Darcy, I want to hear what else my mother has to say!" exclaimed Pattimore. Darcy never flinched but moved straight ahead to sit in the empty chair next to her father.

Mrs. Gilliam continued, "I was so proud to be Pattimore's mom. He was the best thing that ever happened to me," she said as she wiped her eyes. "I have many happy memories with my Pat. I buried him in his favorite blue shirt. I insisted they put it on him even though it was a closed casket. Then I had them slip a small test tube in his shirt pocket so he can continue his science experiments in the afterlife," she sniffled. "He wanted to be a scientist. I didn't want to believe he was dead. I thought the paramedics could save him, but they couldn't"

"That sounds like love and kindness to me, Mrs. Gilliam" said James. "All parents experience denial and hope. Thank you for sharing with us."

James looked around the circle. Mr. Williams had begun to sob and he was concerned more stories might shift the atmosphere in the room to a crying fest. Wanting to move on with the introductions so the parents would leave the first night with a desire to return, James interrupted: "You do not have to always be strong. What is lost cannot be restored. This is not a group of adults who are gathering to cry or hope for a different outcome. I do hope by the end of our sessions that you simply feel better and find peace and acceptance."

James continued. "Recovery is not returning to the way things were before, I mean, that would be magical but there is no going back.

Happiness and anger associated with loss will be discussed, do not hold back. If you feel like crying, then cry. If you want to slam your fist in a metal chair, go ahead!" As he turned back to Mrs. Gilliam, he said, "Thank you for being open and brave. It is time to adjourn for a fifteen-minute break. Would you mind continuing your memories after the break, Mrs. Gilliam?"

"I am fine. Don't break because of me," commented Mr. Williams, feeling guilty for disrupting Mrs. Gilliam. "After I talked about my Darcy, it was like I could feel her presence in the room. It is the first time I have felt her around me"

Darcy jumped to her feet, "*I am in the room, Daddy!*" shouted Darcy. "*I was sitting beside you. Why can't you see me?*"

Pattimore stood and walked toward Darcy and her father. "I explained this, Darcy, we are dead. All five of us in the room are dead!" shouted Pattimore. "Your father cannot hear you so don't lose your cookies. We still don't understand the reason we are all here"

Harry cocking his head to the side. "I understand what you are saying, Pattimore, but why are we here and not…you know…not up there?" He said pointing a chubby finger toward the ceiling.

"I haven't figured that out yet, Harry. Maybe it is a time warp, a purgatory, or a really vivid dream?" said Pattimore.

"I am not dreaming," said Darcy, smiling. "It is a chance to see my pops again so I don't care about the reasons."

Five Spirits

Derek the athletic one started pacing and making a fist with his hands. "Listen you guys, there are weird things going on in this room, and I for one do not want to be here!" said Derek.

"Don't you want to see what happens? I mean my mom is here, your mom is here so maybe it is a surprise party or something," said Harry.

"This is no surprise party, Harry; more like *this was your life* party. Don't you get it?" asked Aaron shaking his head.

"I never had a party; too many germs and I get sick. That is what my mom always told me" Harry said sadly.

"You never had a birthday party?" asked Derek stopping.

"Hush, you guys! I am trying to pay attention!" Darcy.exclaimed.

James paused and smiled at Mr. Williams. "Have you never felt the presence of your daughter around you, like she was in the room or felt like she was sitting next to you?"

"I can't explain it. I was embarrassed to tell anyone about it. Macho men do not see ghosts or spirits. Darcy left us so unexpectedly I still find myself waiting for her to walk in the door. But tonight, I really feel she is here, sense her all around me" said Darcy's father. "And… I am not embarrassed to admit it!"

"It can be a normal, natural thing to feel your child around you, Mr. Williams," responded James. "No embarrassment or judgment. She very well may be sitting next to you at this very moment. I have heard many parents tell me the feeling of their child's presence is very strong.

Some believe in signs from their child like a red cardinal, yellow butterfly or a drgonfly. I personally have felt my son around me several times," said James. "It is not something to be embarrassed about. It is something to celebrate"

Darcy flashed a satisfying smile. "It is as though this James guy can see me or something. If it is possible for our parents to feel our presence, that makes me super happy right now, "said Darcy.

Pattimore huffed. "It can't be scientific. I have never read about it in any of my science books."

Twisting her lips disapprovingly, Darcy snarled at Pattimore. "Just because it has not happened to you, or it's not listed in an encyclopedia does not mean it is not real, Pattimore"

"Let us all take a short break" James commented as the room got quiet. "Feel free to snack on some cheese and crackers. I put it out just before the meeting, fresh. Please trust in the process, eat the snacks, drink the coffee, and talk about your children. In the end, you will understand why you were all chosen for this particular group," said James.

Harry's mother was the first to the snack table and loaded her plate. "I never had dairy in the house. My Harry was allergic to it, so you know how mothers make sacrifices," Ms. Thomas said. "I see no harm in trying a little now."

"I think I will have some too," replied Ruth, Pattimore's mother.

Five Spirits

Pattimore stood on his tip toes watching his mother at the snack table. "Look! My mom stopped crying long enough to get some cheese and crackers. That is the snack she made for me at home! I miss home," said Pattimore.

"Me, too…" Derek chimed in.

"My mom is right. I couldn't eat dairy. It gave me monstrous gas," said Harry. "I had the farts for days if I even looked at cheese!"

"Boys always talk about farts. That's just gross," said Darcy as she joined the group again.

"Girls fart, too, ya know!" shouted Harry crossing his arms.

Pattimore chuckled. "Is this getting creepy or weird to anyone else? Not to change the subject from gas and Harry's farts or anything," he snickered, punching Harry's arm. "Just very weird…"

"What is weird is my mom is filling her plate with snacks I was not allowed to eat, yet I am sitting here talking about farts just hoping she will look at me," said Harry.

"No, I mean really strange kind of weird, not food or talking strange, you dummy!" snorted Pattimore.

"Don't call him a dummy, Pattimore!" shouted Darcy.

"I am sorry, Harry, I forgot to be nice. I meant that hearing my mother and listening to the parents talk is making me think something is amiss around here," said Pattimore. "Anyone agree?"

"Only weird thing is the part James said about punching a chair," said Derek. "I punched things all the time, even broke my hand once, didn't hurt, and didn't help. It is an anger thing."

"You broke your hand?" asked Harry.

"That is not the point, Harry. Pay attention!" replied Derek.

Aaron moved closer to the group, stood to face them, and using his finger, he counted pointing at each one of the five including himself and then said. "Listen you guys; what is weird is that we are the Five Spirits in this Room!"

Five Spirits

4~Ghosts?

"Wait a minute! You mean we are ghosts or something, Aaron?" asked Darcy.

"I am not sure ghosts are the correct verbiage," replied Aaron.

"Hold on… I am the only one that is using the big words in this group," laughed Pattimore. "I digress, please continue"

Darcy held up both hands and faced the other four. "Stop! Hear me out. If we are dead like we all agree, then why can I see you four clear as day? Shouldn't we be floating or have white flowing gowns and a halo or something?"

Pattimore adjusted his glasses, pushing them higher on the bridge of his nose. "I think those are called angels. We are spirits, not yet angels. I predict we are in-between life here on earth and heaven – if there is such a thing. Like we have unfinished business here or something."

Derek stepped forward. "Are you saying you are not sure there is a heaven, Pattimore? Because my mom sure told me there was. I mean, we didn't go to church every Sunday even though she told me she went when she was younger with her dad. We're not flying around the room but we could be angels, right?"

"No, Derek. I am saying I am not sure about heaven just like I am not sure why we are here. What I do know is I can see you and the others as if we were living, pals in school, or something. The whole angel in white robes thing is not a documented sure thing," replied Pattimore. "It could be a myth."

Aaron stood scratching his head listening, then took his turn stepping forward. "We can do an experiment. When Pattimore stood in front of his mother, she did not seem to notice him in the flesh but she did have a look on her face as though she felt something. Maybe when our parents get their refreshments during the break, we can all try to poke them or something?" said Aaron.

"Oh, such a great idea Aaron! We will just poke our parents… With what? Our fingers? Dude, I come up to my mom's kneecaps. Short legs are a curse. We need a better plan," commented Pattimore.

Harry perked up and raised his hand as though he was in school asking the teacher a question. "I know! We can sit on their laps and poke them in the eyes!"

"You are a funny little guy, aren't you, Harry?" snorted Pattimore. "I bet you were a hoot at parties."

Shaking his fists in the air Harry grunted out the words "I said I never went to parties!"

Shaking her head like she was in a rock tumbler, Darcy let out a chuckle as she flailed her arms around. "All this talk, I mean bantering back and forth, is making me dizzy. All ghosts don't fly, all angels don't wear white. That stuff is only in the movies. How about a real plan that includes everyone? I personally would rather be bowling than listen to all your kooky ideas."

Derek shook his head and spoke up. "Okay, enough with the plan. If we are not ghosts, then what are we? Our parents cannot see us; they can not hear us apparently, so let's try something else like walking through walls or putting our hand in a fire to see if we feel pain."

"I don't like pain," whispered Harry.

"I don't like fire," whispered Pattimore.

Derek sat in a chair, leaned forward, and propped his head up with his fist. Gritting his teeth, he mumbled. "I didn't mean an actual fire. Geez… give me a break!"

Throwing his hands up in a gesture of surrender, Aaron walked toward his parents who were loading their plates with snacks. Turning toward the others he shouted for them to watch as he thrust his hand out to grab a few crackers off his mother's plate. "See this?" he exclaimed as his hand passed through the plate to the other side, "we are spirits, ghosts, angels, or what ever you want to call it. We could be aliens or shape shifters for all I know. We just have to accept it. We are no longer earthly beings." He finished and walked back to the group. "That is the one thing we know for sure. We know the who, we know the how, we just don't know the why. Why are we here in this room with our parents who cannot see or hear us?" said Aaron.

"I don't know what a shape shifter is," whispered Harry.

"Seriously, Harry, that is all you got out of all tha,t you little turd? Were you living under a rock your whole life?" shouted Aaron.

Derek, still sitting with his head resting on his fist, chuckled and shook his head. "Just give it a rest, Aaron. He didn't watch Sci-Fi flicks like you apparently did. Why not use a real reference like football or something?"

"Okay. Sorry, Harry. We keep getting off track. Imagine you are a woman shape shifter and you shift and change into the queen of England so you can party with royalty for a while then shift back into the woman you previously were. Get it now?" stated Aaron.

"Nope," whispered Harry as he shook his head no side to side.

Pattimore stood up and adjusted his bowtie. "Okay. Before we get out of control and bash the little guy for living a sheltered life, let's list the facts we know. It is more scientific. Something I understand personally is science. We know we are dead. We know how we died. We know we are no longer in pain and we know that Aaron watched way too many movies growing up. Everyone agree?"

"Agree," said Harry.

"Agree," repeated Darcy. "So what does that leave us?"

"Bowling sounded like a good idea. I never went bowling but I watched it on television. We could arrange the chairs to make an alley then roll Pattimore down to knock over the pins," said Harry.

"Oh. now the little guy has jokes?" shouted Pattimore. "Just try to roll me down the aisle. I am game. I will knock all the pins down including the ones attached to your head!"

"Guys, this is seriously annoying and getting us nowhere, but I would definitely love to watch Pattimore being rolled down the lane. What do we use for pins?" said Derek slapping his leg.

Harry jumped up and started pushing the chairs. Derek threw his head back letting out a belly laugh. "Are you serious, little dude?"

Harry stopped and looked back at the others with a questioning glare. "Of course, I was serious about bowling. I never joke about bowling. I had a little plastic set my mother gave me. It was the only game I could play all by myself in the house. Were you not really serious? I mean I got all excited and everything!"

Darcy stood up and started to assist Harry. "We can play a game if you want to, Harry, but I think we were in the middle of a discussion. We have some fun, then we can direct back to the unfinished business. Deal?"

"Okay, but bowling is more fun. I didn't understand that shape shifting stuff Aaron was talking about anyway"

Aaron grabbed a chair and started lining it u next to Darcy and Harry. "Wait. Darcy said it, I think."

"Said what?" asked Darcy grabbing another chair.

"Unfinished business," Aaron responded.

"You could be right, Aaron. If we are not here for any other reason, that leaves unfinished business. I heard you do not move on…to wherever…if you have unfinished business. I saw it in a movie or something. Like we must be here to let our parents know we are okay or to say goodbye or something"

"Yes, I agree with unfinished business. So, we have to figure out what unfinished business," replied Pattimore. "It must be that we need to some how show our parents we are whole again."

"That Harry can run without wheezing, my body is no longer squished between rocks, and Darcy isn't smashed in a car!" shouted Aaron.

Derek stood up raising his hands in a "V" for victory. "I think that is it! I am no longer hurting and Pattimore has his face back. We are here for unfinished business. To listen to our parents and somehow find a way to let them know we are going to be alright. Do we agree?"

"Agree" they all said in unison.

"Only by the way, Aaron, I wouldn't shape shifter to be the queen, I would be the King!" whispered Harry under his breath.

"Let it go, Harry," said Aaron. "Besides, it's your turn to bowl."

"Umm… since we are agreeing, when I was in the closet over there, I saw some exercise balls, we should use them instead and wait until this meeting is over. Agree?" Harry suggested.

"Agree," the rest replied in unison.

5~Happier Times

As the parents returned from a break to get coffee or have a cigarette, James patiently stayed busy straightening the chairs and adding extra tissue boxes. He noticed Harry's mom was the first to take a plate of cheese and crackers that James displayed. James felt the gleam in his eye forming. It was a good feeling seeing Harry's mother let down the walls and enjoy herself.

The atmosphere in the room had relaxed a bit. Parents were sitting back in their chairs and nodding when another was sharing as if they understood what the other was feeling. Compassion was beginning to form a bond from parent to parent. It didn't matter how the death occurred, it mattered that they all felt the sting of grief, the pangs of hopelessness down to their soul. Not what their religion, money, or the size of their house was.

Today, they shared their feelings without judgment. In the groups James visited before, parents tried to bond but it always seemed awkward. There was always a bit of hemming and hawing trying to listen, but you don't care how their granny died. Grannies are lovely but they lived their whole life. Losing a child, no matter how young or old is different than losing granny. That is why this special group was very much needed.

During the break James started another brew on the coffee before he took his seat and began to talk.

Five Spirits

"Remembering the happier times helps us through the grieving process. The night before your child died, you went to bed on top of the world, but after, you feel like the whole world is sitting on your chest. It may seem ridiculous but please let the memories flow. It can be rewarding to tell your story and can help others that hear it. Whatever you want to tell us is just fine. What was your child's favorite color, hobby, or snack? Everything is important. Each year about eight million people suffer the sudden death of a family member or close friend. That is not counting death that is expected from illness, disease, or old age. Grief is not quick and tidy. It is painful so I would like to go around the room and ask each one to share a story or even a few words about the happier times with your loved one. Mrs. Gilliam you were sharing about young Pattimore before the break. Do you feel up to continuing?"

Pattimore's mother pressed her hands against her cheeks and took a cleansing breath before she straightened her back. "Yes, I was about to say that my Pattimore would have finished high school at age eleven. He was just that smart. I was so proud. However, it made me sad at the same time. He didn't have young friends his age. But he wasn't bothered by it. He was a very serious boy. He would rather read a book or do science projects than play."

"Those are wonderful characteristics, Mrs. Gilliam. Although that is wonderful, I want you to tell the group of a fun time you had with Pattimore if you would. Remember to talk as if they were in this very room. What would you want Pattimore to know about how you remember the fun times, Mrs. Gilliam?"

Pattimore, still sitting on the floor with his legs crossed, looked up at the group. "Mom is having a hard time with the subject because she doesn't have any good memories of me. She hated being in the same room with me and complained about my messiness," he huffed.

"Hush ,Pattimore! This may be a clue to your unfinished business. Just try to listen. We should all listen," replied Darcy.

"She just cries. Mom never understood my science projects no matter how many times I explained them," commented Pattimore, slumping down again. "Who doesn't understand science?"

Putting a hand to the side of her face, Pattimore's mother continued. "I guess the first happy time I remember was when he was a baby and I sang to him. Pattimore would curl up in the crook of my arm and look up at me with innocent wonder and curiosity. He seemed to understand every word," sighed Mrs. Gilliam. "Pattimore also had a slight sense of humor, always making fun of my pointy shoes and his favorite color was blue. Just like that beautiful tablecloth you put out. It was like you put his favorite snack on his favorite color just to honor him."

"Whoa! She never told me that before," said Pattimore raising an eyebrow. "She even knew my favorite color?"

"Sounds like you were close to Pattimore," replied James. "Seems there *were* happier times. Always remember and talk about those times when grief rears its ugly head."

Five Spirits

Sitting up a little taller, she proudly remarked, "I just wanted him to be happy and science was what made him happiest. I believe Pattimore would have been a world-renowned scientist one day. I believed in him," said Mrs. Gilliam.

"I am sure he knew deep down how you felt about him. Our children may not know how to express it, but they do love us. Remember that, Mrs. Gilliam," James said warmly.

Noticing Derek's mother responding emotionally to what Pattimore's mother just said, James looked over at her.

"Is there anyone else that would like to share a happier time with their child next? How about you, Mrs. Tenner?" asked James.

Derek huffed when James turned to his mother. "I remember the happier times and I bet my mother does, too!"

"Is this necessary?" asked the man seated next to Mrs. Tenner. "She has been through enough!"

"I would like to speak for myself," Mrs. Tenner announced firmly, ignoring her boyfriend. "We are only sharing happy memories, so I will be fine. No harm in sharing."

The boyfriend huffed and pulled his coat jacket tighter. He fiddled with his fingers. He looked sweaty and annoyed like a cake left out in the rain. Beads of sweat started to form on his brow, and he could not sit still.

"I have never seen my mom stand up for herself before. Go mom!" shouted Derek pumping his fist in the air.

James took a step toward them and addressed him directly before turning toward Derek's mom. "Everyone in this room has experienced more than they ever should have. That is why we are here." Turning toward Mrs. Tenner James smiled kindly. "Happy is the opposite of anger and I have found if we talk about the happier times, it helps us deal with the anger. Please feel free to speak, Mrs. Tenner," said James. The room was quiet as James walked to his chair in the circle and folded his hands in his lap.

Mrs. Tenner squirmed to sit up straight and cleared her throat. She brushed her thick hair back and then folded her hands in her lap before looking up to address the group.

"Derek was a bigger-than-life kid. He was always muscular and athletic. He played little league baseball, football, and all sports, really. Derek had a great sense of humor and loved the color red. He did everything to the extreme and he drove too fast. There were so many memorable times with Derek it is hard to pick just one. However, one time I was watching in the stands when my Derek hit the ball so far out in the field, further than anyone. I was so proud. All the other parents started cheering. After the game he ran up to the stands to hug me tight. He never minded letting everyone know I was his momma."

As his mother began to speak, Derek slowly looked up from staring at the floor. He pushed back his hooded jacket and began to smile keeping his hands in his pockets.

"She is right, you know. I loved to drive fast. I drove like a race car driver at Indy," said Derek proudly. "She knew me well."

"My Derek also had a big heart. He helped strangers if he could. He would give the shirt off his back if someone needed it. His weakness was girls. He was my boy…" Mrs. Tenner's voice trailed off as she finished.

"Wow! I never heard my mom talk like that. Well, I mean she told me she loved me, but she worked all the time. I thought she would be mad at me. I didn't think she loved me anymore. I wish I could tell her I am sorry. I didn't mean to hurt her," commented Derek.

"Hurt her?" asked Darcy as she stepped up next to Derek. "You mean emotionally or physically?"

"I broke her heart" he said shaking his head. "I wasted all my yesterdays and now I am completely out of tomorrows," whispered Derek.

After hearing Derek's profound statement, Darcy asked, "Does hearing your mom speak about you make you wish things could be different?"

"It sure does. But there is no going back," replied Derek.

Derek's mom continued after a brief pause. "Another memory of my son is my adult friends were his friends, too, it seemed. He was always polite when they came around. One time I was having friends over to bake batches of Christmas cookies when all of sudden he busted in the front door inviting us all to get in his car and go see the

Christmas lights around the neighborhood. He had us all laughing. We still talk about that night."

James looked around the room and noticed smiles beginning to appear on the parents faces after hearing the story about the Christmas lights. Nodding his head at the good job Mrs. Tenner did, he asked her a few questions to show the importance of the group.

"If you don't mind, can you tell me if you ever tried to visit any other community group before this one, Mrs. Tenner?"

"Yes, but like you mentioned before, I felt like the odd duck in the room. I had emotions stir up about how my Derek died and imagined the other parents would judge me."

"I understand completely. I, too, felt like the odd duck when visiting other groups. This group is different, I promise you." said James.

As Derek's mother sat back confidently in her seat, James glanced around the room. Talking about the good times seems to be lightening the mood and his greatest wish was for the parents to feel safe to open up.

"We are always encouraged to move on and try to get back to normal," continued James. "Move on from the denial, accept the facts and get on with your life. However, our normal is changed forever."

James paused to watch the response before he continued. "Our life didn't end the day our child died, even though it feels that way and some hoped it would. We are still entitled to a future, good or bad.

Five Spirits

Today the plan is to remember the denial and anger phases but let us each recall a good quality or happy time with our child to break the ice and discover our voice."

Darcy gently touched Derek's shoulder. "Derek, your mom spoke like you were the angel on the top of her tree. You should try to forgive yourself for breaking her heart. Maybe this is your unfinished business." said Darcy.

Derek bowed his head and took a deep breath before he spoke. "I always did try to make Mom happy. Sometimes I failed and sometimes she sparkled while she laughed. She had the best cackling laugh. I just hope she can forgive me. That is all I care about. It seems like she may have already and that is a good thing,"

James decided to continue with the stories from the parents and turned toward Harry's mother next.

Ms. Thomas, would you like to share a good memory about your son, Harry, with the group?"

"I suppose I could try," Ms. Thomas whispered.

"Oh boy! My mom is going to speak. You all need to listen up because I was a great kid!" Harry exclaimed.

"Hush for once, Harry. You are just a little too hyper for a dead boy," commented Aaron.

Harry glanced a side eye over at the other four, then shrugged his shoulders before settling down to listen to his mother speak.

"I do not know where to start," said Harry's mother.

"You can pick any memory and share it," replied James.

Taking a sip of her water then licking her dry lips, Harry's mother continued. "Okay. Well, my Harry was born beautiful with his olive skin and head full of dark hair. Unfortunately, he was also sickly, small, and his lungs were weak. They repaired a small hole in his heart as a newborn and as he aged, he developed breathing troubles," Harry's mother began. "I never married so I am *Miss* Thomas. Melanie Thomas. Harry's father was not involved although he paid his child support occasionally. That may not sound like a good memory but because of his heart and lung troubles, Harry couldn't go to a regular school. I had him home with me. I live in the home my parents left me. I was a single parent and I felt lucky and blessed for my time with him," she paused to wipe her eyes.

Harry thrust his hands in his pockets and sighed. "Sorry, Mom… I guess I wasn't lucky at staying alive," whispered Harry. "Total failure. That is me."

"Nonsense, Harry! Your mom cherished staying at home with you; my mom worked all the time," said Darcy, folding her arms across her chest. "You should be thankful!"

"Please continue, Miss. Thomas," said James, clearing his throat loudly.

"Did that James guy give us a side eye, like he heard us or something? Did anyone else see it?" asked Aaron.

"Please stop talking. My mom is about to tell her happiest memories," snarled Harry. "Darcy is right: I should be thankful and listen to what she has to say."

Aaron shook his head and took a seat next to Pattimore on the floor, then pulled his hoodie over his head.

Melanie Thomas continued after grabbing another tissue. "Harry used to act out plays, so we made a small stage with purple velvet curtains and spared no expense. My happy time was watching Harry pretend to be a King, Captain Hook, or even a superhero – cape and all. During those times, Harry seemed like a normal boy. After play, he needed his medication or breathing treatments. He was always a good sport about it. Those times when he was acting are my fondest memories…" Ms. Thomas said.

Harry's eyes widened as he stepped forward. "I forgot about the medicine and machines. I always had to stop playing just to take medicine. My mother always held my hand during the treatments" he paused looking at his arms and legs. "I feel great now. I guess I am healed or something," whispered Harry.

"We can't feel pain, doofus. We are dead, remember?" commented Pattimore from his seat on the floor.

The other four shot Pattimore a look. Pattimore threw up his hands as if to surrender and ran a finger across his lips as if he was zipping them shut. "I won't say another word."

James noticed a few smiles as one by one they talked about positive memories of their children. He sensed the informal route was best for this group, so James remained in his seat as he spoke. "We have heard from all the parents here tonight except the parents of Aaron Jackson. Would one of you like to express and share a few happy memories about your son?"

Mr. Jackson took a deep breath as his wife looked up at him. "I guess I can go next," he started. "We are a military family. Our Aaron was very tall and loved to play soldier. He would put my boots on and march around the house. I think his favorite color was green"

"It was orange, Dad, I hated green!" Aaron blurted out.

"He was a good big brother to our other son, Gregory. We didn't stay in one place for too long and I think that made him a little sad, but all in all he was a good kid."

James noticed Mrs. Jackson rolling her eyes as her husband finished. He thought it best to give her a chance. "Did you want to share something as well, Mrs. Jackson?" asked James.

Leaning forward Aaron's mother ran her hand through her hair then sat back and crossed her arms defensively across her chest.

"My husband's happy memory was Aaron wearing his boots? Really? It is obvious who was never home and who was the stay-at-home mom. And his favorite color was orange not green!" remarked Mrs. Jackson, stomping her feet on the floor for emphasis. Before Mr. Jackson could comment, James guided Mrs. Jackson to continue.

"Please continue, Mrs. Jackson, and tell us more about your son. Each parent has special memories that the other parent may or may not share," said James.

"That's the truth!" began Mrs. Jackson, the tone of her voice clearly telling her husband he should stay quiet. "Aaron was sensitive, but his father wanted him to be strong and tough. I gave him love and his father gave him a crew cut. I bought him blue jeans, books to read and cowboy boots. His father bought him sensible sneakers and wanted him to play sports. Yes, it sounds like I am angry. I am angry! I want my boy back!" She reached for the box of tissues next to her.

"I cannot lie, what she is saying is the absolute truth. I was different around my mom than I was my dad, but I loved them both," whispered Aaron. "I wish they didn't argue all the time."

"Same with me. I only met my father one time. He complained that I was too pale and that my mother was raising me to be a soft boy, whatever that means," said Harry.

Derek felt the tension rising in the room and turned to the others. "It is different with fathers than mothers. I could work on cars with my dad and watch racing on television. My mother wanted it quiet in the house. I knew how to handle her though, I would just make her laugh by acting goofy, and she would just about pee her pants laughing so hard," said Derek.

"I never saw my mother laugh," commented Pattimore.

"Quit being a Gloomy Gus, Pattimore! I don't understand why, but this seems like an incredible opportunity to hear our parents speak about us. It could go *'poof!'* at any minute and we could disappear as fast as we appeared," commented Darcy.

Aaron, shaking his head in agreement, stepped out in front of the other four to get their attention. "Listen, if we are here to find out and correct some unfinished business, I suggest we listen to our parents talk so we can find clues. Harry's mother said he was sickly, but it didn't matter, she loved his acting and plays. Derek's mom never mentioned the way Derek died, so maybe she has forgiven him and Darcy's parents just want to go fishing. There has to be a clue here somewhere guys."

Derek then stood and took the position in the front, forcing Aaron to move aside. "Okay, so if we are looking for clues to our unfinished business then what will happen after we figure it out is what I want to know."

Speaking from her position on the floor, Darcy smoothed her curls and looked up at Derek. "You are so restless, were you this restless in life…I mean when you were alive?"

"Yes, I couldn't sit still. Hard a hard time sleeping, too, if you want to know the truth. It was like I was always supposed to be doing something or be somewhere I was late to."

"Maybe we can move on, but where will that be and will it be different for each of us? I am just getting used to all of you. I don't want to go anywhere if I have to go alone," said Harry.

"Listen, guys… We are all still here, so we haven't figured it out yet. This may take more time -- like the whole five weeks that James guy mentioned. Don't panic. We can figure this out," replied Pattimore.

James waited for Mrs. Jackson to grab a tissue and compose herself before he continued. He knew parents kept their feelings bottled up inside until they exploded like a bomb. He knew all too well that the anger stage can rear its ugly head at anytime during the grieving stage. It is mostly caused by one parent never having the chance to express subdued emotions for fear of offending their partner.

He let Aaron's parents settle back down before he spoke again to the group. "It is better to scream it out than to hold it in, because holding back your feelings is like dancing to music no one else can hear. You are alone in the waltz your partner never knew existed."

The first meeting of the Secret Good-byes group had gone well, and James was pleased that all parents managed to speak at least once to share a good memory about their child. He was looking forward to the next week even though the topic would be anger, the second stage of grief. James cleaned the coffee pot inside and out, replacing it back in the machine. Next, he took off the blue tablecloth and folded it carefully.

James walked over to the bag he brought to all the meetings and pulled out a new cloth for the table, replacing the blue one with a soft yellow one. He took care to smooth out the wrinkles then stood back to give it a look. Satisfied that everything was in place, snacks stored away and tissue boxes placed, James put on his coat. Tucking the dirty tablecloth under his arm to take home and clean, he headed to the door. James turned out the lights to the community center and paused at the door for only a brief moment.

"One meeting down and four more to go," he whispered to himself. Then he locked the door to the community center and went home to relieve the nurse watching over his wife for the night.

"What do we do now?" asked Aaron, looking puzzled.

"I guess we wait or sleep or something," claimed Pattimore.

"I don't feel a bit sleepy; I feel amazing!" said Harry.

"I know we can't leave," said Darcy. "I tried to follow my daddy to keep him company, but I couldn't get past the doorway."

"I am really nervous about being stuck here," replied Aaron. "I have been stuck before; and it did not end well."

While the others were talking amongst themselves, Darcy approached the snack table and ran her fingers on the yellow cotton tablecloth. "Yellow is my favorite color. One year my mother dressed me up on Easter in a yellow flowered dress. It went well with my hair color. Why do you think that James guy changed the tablecloth?" asked Darcy glancing at the others.

"Who cares? Maybe the other one was dirty?" said Aaron.

"Maybe he has a thing for bananas," laughed Harry.

"Settle down, hyper Harry," Pattimore teased.

"It is hard to sit still, Pattimore, I don't feel sick anymore. Do any of you feel different like I do?" asked Harry.

"Nope," said Pattimore looking down at his legs. "I am still short, nothing changed here."

"So funny, Pattimore. There is more to life than how tall you are. I mean… I feel like doing cartwheels or something. I feel strong and whole. I am not wheezing and turning blue around the lips. Doesn't anyone else feel whole like they have been gifted a new body?" asked Harry.

Aaron examined his arms, patted his stomach, and began to smile as his blue eyes brightened. "Come to think of it, my arms can move and my stomach doesn't hurt or feel squished" replied Aaron.

"Squished… Ewww, yuck! Why would you feel squished, Aaron?" asked Harry.

"I died by being crushed between two large boulders, Harry, but thanks for bringing attention to how we are now made whole. I have no more pain either!" replied Aaron. "Is this normal for people who have died?"

"I hadn't noticed until just now, but I can move my arms and my chest doesn't hurt!" claimed Darcy. "This is amazing"

"What about you, Derek?" asked Harry, looking at Derek.

Derek gave himself a glance from head to toe then checked both arms and nodded while shifting his weight from side to side. Rubbing his neck all around then shaking his head like he was shaking water from his ears. "I suppose I am alright. I don't feel pain now. I don't remember feeling pain when I died either. It was more like not being able to breathe. It only lasted a minute, and then I was floating," said Derek. "Like some of you said earlier, floating was nice. Peaceful, even."

Pattimore stood up, joining the others as they examined their bodies. "I really don't remember pain either. I mean I think I remember mixing chemicals one minute then I don't remember anything," commented Pattimore. "How is that possible?"

Derek tilted his head to the side. "I don't have an answer for that, little dude. For me, my passing was peaceful. That is what had me thinking. It was all over in a nanosecond. However, I can see the pain in my mother's face and it makes me feel her sadness. She is the one in pain now and I am feeling fine. Is there a way to let her know I am okay, I wonder?" asked Derek. "Maybe *that* is my unfinished business. I need to let my mother know I am okay! I am not suffering one bit."

Aaron wrinkled his nose, then cupping his elbow with one hand, he began tapping his lips with the other. "I think we all can agree that we love seeing our parents but hate knowing they are hurting. I for one am hopeful that our parents are going to be okay without us. If we could find a way to do that, then maybe we would not be stuck in this room any longer," said Aaron. "Besides, there has to be a reason we are here, so maybe it is so we can let them know we are okay and they can stop worrying."

Pattimore pushed his glasses up on his nose as he stood in front of the other four. "There is an emotional conflict going on here. I think Aaron has a good hypothesis. The five of us may be stuck here because of the need to make sure our parents will be okay. So perhaps we need to find a way to show them. That is possibly all of our unfinished business! Anyone have any suggestions?"

After another lap around the room, Harry stopped in front of the group. "If my mom could see me run without wheezing, she would know I am going to be fine. I am feeling amazing right now," said

Harry. "I just can't stop running. It feels so good to run. I wish my mom could see me now!"

"Are you saying that you have never gone on a run or a hike, Harry?" asked Darcy.

"No, not ever. I lived in a bacteria-free, dust-free environment so my lungs would not get sick. Now I feel like I am prancing to the finish line," replied Harry.

"Well, prance on, little dude. I don't suppose it can hurt you now, seeing as we are all dead," commented Derek. "I do agree with Aaron about wanting to let our parents know we are alright and pain free. I think it would help a whole lot. They may find some peace in knowing we are fine, even better. No pain, bad thoughts, or anger"

Grimacing as he watched Harry run around the room, Pattimore raised his eyebrows. "Wait, Harry. How you were living in a bacteria free house is what I want to know. Because you know… I am a scientist," asked Pattimore.

"Easy. My mom had men come and wrap the living room in plastic. They covered the windows so dust would not come in. Anything I touched had to be wiped down with a special solution. It was crazy but all I ever knew. Doesn't anyone else know what I am talking about?" asked Harry. "I was allergic to everything!"

Derek laughed slinging his head back. "Sorry, buddy, I lived in the country. I rarely wore shoes unless to go to school. I ran barefoot in the yard, got sandspurs stuck in my feet, worked on cars, climbed trees, built fires, and did everything with no shirt on. I was raised a country boy and I loved it," said Derek.

"Wow! I have only seen a tree through plastic from my window. You climbed a tre,e Derek? That must have been so cool," said Harry.

Aaron pulled out a chair and sat down, leaning back gazing at the group. He folded his arms and stretched out his long legs. "We all lived different lives before we died. I was raised in the city. We had a large five-bedroom house. I played neighborhood football and played kickball in the streets. When a car was coming, we would all yell *'Car!'* then you knew to get out of the road. I had name-brand clothes and the best kicks money could buy. I hated school, I hated living in the city, and I hate that I snuck away and took a road trip with my friends without my parents permission." Feeling the heaviness of it all, Aaron began to be less boisterous. "We cannot go back. There has to be a reason. That reason may be to make sure our parents are dealing with our death."

Putting a finger in the air, Pattimore paced back and forth in front of the group. "Maybe it is not about us at all. Perhaps we are not here to prove we are okay but that our parents are going to be okay. We are here to listen to our parents so we can hear all the things they wanted to say before we died but didn't get the chance to."

"What do you mean, Pattimore?" asked Derek.

Pattimore explained, "For example, you died not knowing how your mother felt. I died not knowing how my mother felt about my science experiments and Harry here thought he was a pain in the butt with all his plastic covered windows and medications. So… I am saying this could be our unfinished business. We need to hear about the love."

Derek plopped in the chair and rubbed his chin. "I see what the little dude is saying but apparently we have to listen for five weeks, so I suggest we make a pact to listen, so we discover the unfinished business and get out of here."

Aaron turned the chair nearest Derek and straddled it. "I agree, but there has to be more to it than that. My parents argued and my mother was embarrassed. I did hear some love but this may be why they are here for five meetings. It might take that long to talk everything over. We should find a way to speed up the process. I am going batty in here."

"You could run around the room with me Aaron. Or we could have a race!" laughed Harry.

Darcy had been leaning against the wall listening as the boys debated over finding out the next page in the book of dying. She strolled out to the middle of the community center and opened her arms wide. "I don't think complaining, planning or debating why we are dead or why we are here is the answer. We are now free of pain, free of anger and free from the demands of our former lives. I say that we all think of a way to communicate with our parents and try it out at the next meeting. Like sitting next to them and hugging them until they feel we are here with them. Everyone agree?" asked Darcy. "Right now, I just want to twirl."

"Agree," said Aaron.

"Agree," said Derek.

"Pattimore? What do you say?" asked Harry.

"Okay, I agree to try, but it is not scientific, just saying…" replied Pattimore. "Did I mention I wanted to be a scientist?"

As they all five stood in the center of the room and began to twirl with their arms opened wide, Darcy stopped to look down at Pattimore. Darcy leaned down so her face was just at his. "The bow tie makes you look like an adorable boy, but you are an ornery little dude, Pattimore," said Darcy. "Just twirl and keep quiet!"

7~Blame Game

As the next Wednesday approached for the second meeting of the group, James looked over his plans as the parents filed in and took their seats. James carefully planned each night down to the color of the tablecloths and snacks to invoke the stirring of certain feelings and familiar emotions attached to their child. Having prepped the coffee, placed the tissue boxes, and added donuts to the refreshment area, he was ready to welcome the parents. James noticed a few parents greeting each other with smiles of familiarity on their faces and a few handshakes. *"This is progress,"* he thought to himself, *"the plan is working."* Standing, James addressed the parents as they settled into their seats.

"This is our second of five meetings. It is wonderful to see that everyone returned and I see that Mrs. Williams, Darcy's mother, Nanette, has joined us. We welcome you to the group!"

Mrs. Williams was a curvy woman with dark curly hair and a splattering of freckles that made her look younger than she was.

Darcy stood up from her spot on the floor and began to clap her hands. "My mother came! Daddy is not alone tonight!" Darcy said beaming with pride seeing both her parents sitting next to each other.

"I had obligations I had to attend to last week, but my husband came home giving me a full report. You can call me Nan, short for Nanette. I am glad to be here," Mrs. Williams replied.

"No worries. Glad to have you. Now let's begin… The second stage of grief is anger and we only brushed the surface last week," James began. "With anger comes the blame game. One parent may blame the other; you might blame a doctor, or even blame your child. Blame is natural. Don't beat yourself up over it," he chuckled.

All five of the spirits had gathered on the floor facing the parents in the circle determined to listen for clues of their unfinished business.

"I know who I would blame," blurted Harry.

"Who?" asked Pattimore, straightening his bow tie?

"The doctor for giving me all that medicine," replied Harry. "I never wanted to take it. I wanted to be normal."

"Everyone's normal is different, Harry," said Darcy. "I am sorry you lived in a bubble, but I am sure it was to keep you safe. That was normal for you. I lived with my parents and that was my normal. Your mom did the best she could. Don't beat yourself up over it like James said just now."

"Good point, Darcy," replied Harry.

James allowed a long pause for the information to sink in and watched as everyone squirmed a little in their chairs.

"We are all learning to navigate grief. There is no blueprint for the emotions that surge through your body. The whole world seems unfair. You look at other people in cars, at restaurants or in the neighborhood and wonder why they look so normal. They don't know that your personal world has been turned upside down," continued James. "Anyone feel that way?"

As the group nodded almost in unison, James moved over to an empty chair in the circle. He hoped to keep the comfortable tone in the room. "Tonight, we are going to go around the room and all say a quick good memory again, like we did last week then move on to anger the second stage of grief and include blame. Who did you blame for the death of your child? Blame is the fuel of anger. Like gasoline on a fire. It is something to be addressed. What better place to do that then right here in this group with parents who can relate? There are worse things than grief and anger even though it may seem never ending. Grief isn't the enemy, numbness is. Don't become numb. Let us talk about it. Who wants to go first?"

Turning his back on the group "I don't want to hear this," commented Derek. "I don't want to hear how mad my mom is about my death. This can't be good."

"I think they have to get through this part to move on or something. I don't think I want to hear it either. I don't want to know about their anger," replied Darcy.

"I like hearing what our parents have to say," commented Aaron. "Things they should have said to us when we were alive, I suppose. Let out their guilt. Maybe they will say something we want to hear."

"I pictured the city boy would be a suck up. None of us want to hear the bad but with the bad comes the good, so be quiet," replied Darcy. "My mother taught me that."

Mrs. Williams glanced around the room then raised her hand. "Since I missed last week, I would love to say something positive about my daughter, Darcy, first before we jump into the anger if that is okay?"

"Yes, Mrs. Williams, go right ahead. Remember we want to talk as though our children are in the room listening. It is important," said James.

"Well, please call me Nan. I am Darcy's mother. We lost her at age nineteen. She was a young unmarried mother herself. We are now taking care of her daughter, Roberta. My best memory of Darcy is playing dress-up and singing like she was a rock star. She wanted to be a singer or movie star. I wore a uniform, and she would put it on and pretended to be me sometimes"

"I can't believe she said that," declared Darcy. "It is actually what I wanted to be. Sort of embarrassing, really."

"As if privacy matters now that we are dead," commented Aaron.

"I think it is a cute and happy memory," chuckled Harry. "I imagine you were cute playing dress-up. Don't be embarrassed."

"Just wait until it is my mother's turn. She will probably talk about when I was in diapers," huffed Pattimore.

"Just hush, you guys. Some of us want to listen," scolded Derek. "Anything they say positive about us is a good thing. After all, we let them down, didn't we?"

"I never thought of that," said Darcy. "We did let them down, so how are they ever going to forgive us?"

Nan Williams cleared her throat and continued. "I suppose when I got angry, I blamed just about everyone. I blamed her ex, the truck driver that she ran into, God, and even Darcy. I got annoyed with her like any mother would, but I would change it all if I could have her back singing into a hairbrush like she was famous. She made her choices. She is not to blame; I just wasn't ready to bury my child."

"Thank you, Nan. That was very brave of you to share that with us. Nothing can prepare us for when life breaks our heart," replied James. "Putting the hurt and blame aside is difficult."

Pausing long enough for the parents to gain their composure, James looked around the room for who might speak next. Usually, they give a subtle sign like squirming in their chair or licking their dry lips in preparation. His eyes stopped on Aaron Jackson's mother who was upstaged by Mr. Jackson last week.

"Mrs. Jackson, would you like a turn to tell us a positive about your son, Aaron, then just merge into anger and blame when you feel comfortable," explained James.

"This ought to be good… My mom and I were close. Closer than my dad who was always away being a soldier," commented Aaron crossing his arms in anticipation.

"I am Rebecca Jackson, the mother of Aaron Jackson. Aaron loved to bake cookies with me and loved family dinners around the table. I hold on to those good memories that he and I shared. That is what gets me through." Mrs. Jackson cleared her throat and continued, "However, Aaron got into a bad crowd. Then Aaron went missing, we thought he had run away. I blamed my husband for pushing the military too hard. I blamed the police for not finding him in time to save him, and of course I blamed Aaron."

She continued, "After a month, Aaron was found in the desert, wedged between two rocks. His lungs were crushed. He had tried to climb a rock ledge and fell thirty feet. I was in denial until I demanded to see the body. It was my Aaron. His face was still the handsome son I loved, and he looked peaceful as though he was sleeping. I was so angry. He should have come to me, talked to me. If he was in the room, I would want him to know…I would have done anything for him." She finished and wiped her eyes. "Anything…"

Aaron scrambled to his feet watching his mother's expression. "*I am so sorry, Mom. You got it all wrong. I didn't run away, really. I had forgotten about the cookies we baked and never told dad. I didn't mean to hurt you!*" shouted Aaron.

"Listen, Aaron. Your mom said nice things about you," said Harry. "She knows you loved her."

The other four gathered in a huddle around Aaron. "There is no going back but now you know," said Pattimore. "At least *you* know!"

"Hey, maybe that is why we are all stuck here!" shouted Derek. "Hearing what our parents have to say is like penance or something."

"If only I knew how she felt, I would not have left. I just wanted to have fun. Mom was always trying to protect me," replied Aaron.

James straightened his back and placed his hands on his knees. "We need a little break and then how about we hear from Derek's parents again? We are talking about blame and we all have blamed someone, even ourselves. Are you interested in taking your turn after the break, Mrs. Tenner?"

James deliberately focused on Derek's mother after seeing her shift in her seat. Blame is uncomfortable followed by regret. He understood fully how people and marriages often do not survive the death of a child. Blame, guilt, and anger are the enemies. His own wife stopped talking to him then disappeared in to the dark places in her brain. James shuddered at the vision of his wife's mental state.

Aaron took his seat with the other four and folded his hands in his lap. "That was hard to hear, but I needed to hear it, I guess. Maybe Derek is right: this is our punishment."

After a break for donuts and coffee refills James asked everyone to take their seats to allow Mrs. Tenner the opportunity to speak.

Five Spirits

"Mrs. Tennerr, please tell us your fond memory then dive gently into the anger and blame. I'll remind you as I did everyone: please speak as though your son is listening."

"Hello, I am Carol, the mother of Derek. From the time he was very young, he loved for me to scratch his head. It started as a nightly routine and continued on. Anytime he had an issue or was tired he came and laid his head in my lap and we talked the problem through. I thought we were close, and he trusted me," she gulped. "It came a time when I had to practice tough love. I pushed him away. You see my Derek dipped his toe in the drug scene. A girlfriend got him started. One day when he was stressed out, high on drugs and arguing with his girlfriend, my Derek took his own life," said Mrs. Tenner. "I just don't understand why. He was so loved."

"I know how difficult this is for you but please, for your emotional health, try to continue Carol," James encouraged.

"Oh, my god! You killed yourself, Derek?" asked Darcy.

"Leave him alone!" screamed Aaron. "He needs to hear what his mother has to say. No one knows his story but him. We all did something to cause our death. I did something stupid that caused my death. We cannot judge, we don't know his story"

James rushed to bring Mrs. Tenner a cup of water. She took a few sips and nodded that she wanted to finish.

"I was so angry when I got the call. I blamed his father, his girlfriend, and myself. I should have been there. I was not equipped to deal with this situation. Now he is gone, and I don't know if he realizes just how much he meant to me. I miss him down to my very soul," she finished.

Staring straight ahead, in a monotone voice Derek spoke not just to the other four but to himself as well. *"I knew, Mom. I am right here, Mom. I felt the love you had for me and I also knew how much I hurt you. I wish I could take it all back. I regret my decision. You were the best mom ever and I am so thankful that you were chosen to be my mom,"* commented Derek. *"It was my decision, not yours, and not your fault,"*

Derek stood up, still staring straight at his mother. "I am going to hug her and hope she feels my presence."

The other four spirits in the room watched as Derek stood behind his mother and wrapped his arms around her. Mrs. Tenner closed her eyes and leaned back in her chair as though she knew her son was present. James gave a pause before speaking.

"Are you alright, Mrs. Tenner?" asked James.

"Yes, I am fine. Often times I can feel my son around me and this is one of those times," Mrs. Tenner replied. "I know he is here."

"They can actually feel us in the room?" asked Harry.

"I guess they can. I am going to hug my mom, too!" declared Darcy, running toward her mom.

Soon four out of the five spirits were standing behind their parent, wrapping their arms around them in a loving embrace. Pattimore stood up watching the others, then plopped down on the floor and put his head in his hands.

"I don't think I can. I am not as sure as you all are that my mom is going to be okay," said Pattimore.

"I …I would like to go next please," remarked Ms. Gilliam in a soft voice. "If it is okay."

"You are welcome to speak next. Then all we have left is the mother of Harry Thomas," said James giving a kind smile. "Speak as if your children were wrapping their arms around you right now"

"Wait…can that guy see us?" asked Harry.

"I don't know," replied Darcy. "It is kind of creepy."

"How could he possibly know we are hugging our parents right now?" replied Aaron.

"This James dude has secret powers," laughed Harry.

"Do you have a mute button, Harry?" laughed Derek. "I am sure it is just a coincidence or a good guess."

Pattimore's mother smoothed her dress and sat up straight. "Pattimore was a preemie baby," started Mrs. Gilliam. "I didn't know if he would survive because he was so tiny. His father couldn't handle it, so he left us at the hospital, packed his belongings, and left that day"

"Mom, stop telling our business. Just go back to crying!" shouted Pattimore.

"Pattimore, she cannot hear you," remarked Harry.

Pattimore pulled at his bowtie nervously and adjusted his glasses. "What is the point of all this anyway? I will never grow up; I will never learn to drive and never be a scientist," growled Pattimore.

"I think we are meant to hear the things they always thought we already knew but never got the chance to tell us. If that makes any sense. Our parents thought we understood what they meant when they told us we couldn't do something. It was assumed we loved them and knew they loved us," commented Derek. "It is complicated being a kid. Let's stop talking and listen more. I like the listening better at this point. I don't want to think."

Pattimore's mother pushed herself to continue. "Pattimore was small in stature but big on brains," continued Mrs. Gilliam. "Pattimore could read a full chapter book by age four. He did science experiments with items I could not pronounce right in our kitchen. I bought him a chemistry set when he was six. His little face doing experiments is my happy memory of him," she paused.

Pattimore's mother looked down at her pointy shoes and began wringing her hands nervously. Sitting up again, she pushed the bridge of her glasses back with one finger then smoothed her skirt. "As Pattimore progressed, he was asked to move to an advanced class. Math and Science came so easy to him. I couldn't read, so I just signed the papers saying it was okay to move him up. I often think it was too much for him. Maybe he should have stayed with kids his age. That was when the bullying started"

Five Spirits

"My own mother could not read. I never knew that. I thought she was ignoring me," remarked Pattimore. "Any more of the truth coming out of her mouth and I might haunt her the rest of my days."

"Try to listen, Pattimore. You might learn your mom had a hard life, but she did the best she could for you," Darcy commented.

"I told you I am listening, but it is almost too embarrassing," said Pattimore. "I usually prefer to keep my feelings hidden"

"I find that unbelievable," replied Harry.

Pattimore reached over and started rubbing Harry's back and pretended to search all over him lifting his arms.

"What are you doing, Pattimore?"

Pattimore sat back down on the floor and sternly looked at Harry. "I am searching for that mute button. It has to be here somewhere!"

"Very funny, Pattimore" Harry retorted.

Pattimore's mother continued. "Just before high school graduation, Pattimore was working on a big experiment. He asked for extra money to buy chemicals and other stuff so he could really impress the teachers at the school. I sold a piece of jewelry to get the money he insisted he needed to do the big experiment properly"

Mrs. Gilliam paused to blow her nose and folded her hands calmly back in her lap before she continued. "Pattimore decided that it would be best if he tried the experiment at home first before he took it to school. I usually gave in to his demands. Probably because he was my only child. The day of the first trial of the experiment he asked me…

no, he demanded that I leave him alone. I went to my room. I was in my room watching soap operas when I heard the explosion. I lost my Pattimore. It was especially tragic to his sweet face. I didn't have the money to hire someone to clean up so after he was pronounced dead at the hospital I came home and got a bucket and scrubbed until my hands were raw. My landlord evicted me and I live in a shelter now. I blame myself. I am the one to blame."

"I did not know all that happened," whispered Pattimore. "She lives in a shelter because of me and my experiments?"

"You couldn't have known she would be evicted Pattimore. We don't know what happens after we leave or what our parents went through," said Derek. "There is no crystal ball."

"I know now," said Pattimore. "I feel so bad. This is penance! I was blissfully ignorant on how I died until now. Geez I blew myself up? I wish my mom could hear me…" "*Mom, I am sorry, but geez, if you do not like where you are then move, you are not a tree!*"

James rubbed his hands together and looked at the floor. "I know it was a difficult story to tell, Mrs. Gilliam," said James. Noticing some parents were touched by Mrs. Gilliam's story as they avoided eye contact, he allowed time to consume the gravity of it all.

Turning in his chair, he looked over at Harry's mother. "Can we hear your story now, Ms. Thomas? We are almost out of time."

Melanie Thomas sat on the edge of her chair, her back straight and tall. She was unbreakable, like a lone sequoia in a forest, and shook her head. "I can't talk about it yet. Everyone telling their story has made me so upset. Each story different, but with the same tragic ending."

Melanie had a hard time looking up. She rocked and hugged her purse until the vinyl crinkled. The picture of her son was in there. She took it everywhere, pulling it out when she needed to be reminded of his sweet face.

"That is alright, Ms. Thomas. Maybe you can one day," replied James. "Talking about the anger and blame stage is the hardest."

"No one knows my horrid details and I am not sure I want to share them. I am the boat in the moat, just circling the castle going nowhere" said Ms. Thomas. "I think some things are better kept to myself, untold and unshared."

"This is the time and place to let it all out, even the horrid details. It can be harmful to keep it all inside, which is the purpose of coming to the meetings. Our emotions can change with incredible speed and only you have the ability to put on the emotional brakes. In here, we can let it all out. Free our insides from the tornado that is churning in our mind. You were handpicked for this group. All of you were chosen to be here. I chose each of you to help you heal," James said.

Looking emotionally drained, Harry's mom continued. "My story is not special; it is criminal and makes me angry to talk about it. I prefer to let others go first. I don't want to fumble over my words," said Ms. Thomas.

James nodded towards her, not wanting to push her too hard. "After the shock of the death, the funeral, and saying the habitual '*thank you for your kind words and prayers*,' it is hard to sit in the silence that follows. You think over and over of the events in your head. Did this really happen to me? What could I have done differently?"

As James began to pace, he rubbed his chin recalling how he asked himself those very same questions. He looked down at his shoes as he paced, trying to hide any outburst of emotions. This was not the time to break down although it still flooded his mind unexpectedly without warning. He went through a time where he held it all in. Sarah refused to talk to him, and he felt lonely yet agitated at the same time. The pacing was bringing it all back, so he sat back down in his seat, crossed his legs, and took a deep breath before speaking frankly to the group.

"Sometimes you want to talk about all the details, but you get angry at yourself for thinking that way. Telling yourself it would not be right to talk about such things, so you suck it in, bite your lip. Your child existed, yet when you start to talk about it, others just turn away because they fear they will upset you, but honestly, we need to talk. Here, in this group you can talk about anything and everything down to the tiniest detail. Right down to the blood splatter on the walls if that is what you need to do. The paleness of their skin when you saw them in the morgue or their blue lips. It is not to get sympathy or a helping hand. It is just a need to talk. There are no limitations to your grief, it is endless. So let your sharing or talking about your particular loss be endless as well."

James again paused and looked over at the parents in the room. Their eyes were focused on him. He could sense they wanted to talk about all the details with someone. He saw relief in their eyes and determination as they stiffened up in their chairs relieved to be given such a permission to divulge their innermost thoughts.

Clasping his hands together James leaned back in his chair and looked up at the ceiling. "With endless love, comes endless grief," he announced. "You can get to that final stage of acceptance. Some grip it naturally, and some need a big push. In this group you will welcome that push. Well maybe a nudge, but I promise you will see with your eyes and feel with your heart that there is a way to live on. I think that is all for tonight. Remember you are stronger than your pain. I look forward to seeing you all next week."

8~Home

After all the parents left the community center James started to clean out the coffee pot washing the glass carafe carefully. He then bagged up the left-over snacks. He placed the snacks in the cupboard to share the leftovers with the next group coming into the community center. Alcohol Anonymous was scheduled for the following night and he was happy to share.

James also liked to take his time to prolong going home. The nurse did not leave until nine o'clock in case his class ran long, so there was still plenty of time. Even though he tried hard to prepare himself on the long drive home, he knew what he would see and how sad he would be when he arrived. It was the same day by day.

When his child, Joshua, died that morning, he and his wife had experienced a long night of arguing the day before. It was just like all the arguments they had before but this time there was yelling, slamming of doors, and cursing. James thought it would blow over and he would just shake it off like dog poop on his shoe, but unlike all the other times this uneasy feeling continued well into the next day. This was the first argument they brought up their son and his care in their loud discussion. He regretted it immediately. He just knew Joshua had to have known and heard most of the yelling through the walls.

When the news came that Joshua was found dead, the denial stage came and went fast turning the page from denial to anger. James embraced the anger stage with such vigor that it nearly broke his wife into pieces. The pieces that can never be put back together once they are shattered. James was vicious with his accusations even when his wife crumbled to the floor sobbing. The anger bubbled inside of him like a volcanic eruption he could not control. Recalling the fuss about who should be the last to leave the house to ensure Joshua got on the bus resonates in his ears so loud it kept him from sleeping.

James insisted he was the breadwinner and his job was more important, so he arose earlier than usual and headed out the door to avoid any issues and honestly just trying to be the first one out the door. His wife, Sarah, who he thought was still sleeping, had done the same thing. Sarah was picked up by an office carpool but decided to take her car from the garage and left early while James was in the shower. He never thought to look for her car in the garage. Joshua was left alone to make his own lunch and get himself to the bus stop.

No one was there to make sure he wore a coat. No one was there to make his breakfast or tie his shoes. In his heart James knew they were both to blame but he lashed out on his wife for changing the routine, for slipping out without a care or concern for Joshua. Sarah had a complete mental breakdown and spent a year in a mental facility until James finally forgave her and brought her home to care for her. "Till death do us part," he always said.

Eventually quitting his job, James began volunteering at the community center. He was still in a state of anger at Sarah and mourning for Joshua until one day he was asked to sit in on a grief counseling class that changed his life forever. James learned from the class but was disappointed that there were no classes created just for parents who lost a child. He wanted to create a class just for angel parents, but he did not know where to start. He had all but given up.

James did not come by this idea of a special group all on his own. Every night when he came home from work after the death of his son he would sit on the end of Joshua's bed, pick up his toys, run his hands on the bedcovers that were still in the same position as Joshua had left them, and sob uncontrollably. It was a routine and it was a release for James. After his nightly routine in Joshua's room, he would wipe his eyes, blow his nose, and then force himself to visit his wife in the other room. James forgave his wife daily for leaving their son and every night he spent time honoring their son. It was a routine that gave him a few moments of bravery to face the sleepless night ahead.

When he realized Sarah would never recover, James moved his belongings and slept in the spare room. The master bedroom had been turned into a mental health room for his wife, complete with hospital bed, oxygen tanks, and a pharmacy that would make a druggist uncomfortable. Nurses were hired to sit with his wife for twelve hours a day and he took the night shift trying to keep from emptying their savings. He even closed out the college fund they started for Joshua.

After a year, James tried to take on odd jobs to keep the nurses and equipment required to take care of Sarah at home. Insurance had maxed out and their savings were gone. Sarah, who once walked with the encouragement of the nurse's aides, had now taken to her bed in the fetal position the last few years. She was being fed through a tube and had been placed in diapers. James loved Sarah but he knew that love wasn't enough to save Sarah. She had retreated to a small dark room deep in her brain and was never going to return. Money was getting low, and James had but a few choices left.

One particular night after spending an hour in his son's room he made up his mind on what he had to do. He glanced around the room and chose Joshua's favorite toy. A twelve-inch tyrannosaurus rex. Joshua loved dinosaurs. He could name them all, but the T-Rex was his favorite. Tucking the stuffed toy under his arm he entered Sarah's room. James placed the dinosaur on the pillow next to Sarah then went to the medicine cabinet and began gathering as much morphine as he could. He secretly had been hoarding the syringes full of morphine from the nurses so he would have enough. One for Sarah and one for him. He pulled back the plunger on the syringes and filled them to 50cc. James located the intravenous tube going into Sarah's veins and stuck the first needle in the port. Before he pushed the plunger, he looked over at Sarah one last time. The dinosaur was no longer on the pillow where he placed it. It seemed to have disappeared. As he looked around the room, he spotted the favorite toy next to the wall and went to retrieve it. Coming back to the bedside James sat on the edge pushing the hair from Sarah's face. Thrown off by the toy being moved he leaned in close. Her hair smelled like her strawberry shampoo. It was the one thing he insisted on when the nurse showered her. Her skin was getting paler with every day Sarah was deprived of sunshine.

"Sarah, can you hear me? Did you throw Joshua's dino across the room, you naughty girl?"

He looked at her and leaned in to kiss her on the cheek. Sarah never moved. Feeling confused, he put the dinosaur next to Sarah again and lifting her elbow, he tucked the dino in the crook of her arm. Draping her arm around the neck of their son's favorite toy.

"I want a part of Joshua to be here with us. I want him to comfort us" whispered James. "Don't you want him here, too?"

James stood to check the IV and heard a thump. As he turned, he noticed the dinosaur was again missing from the bed. A cold feeling swept over him as he looked at the toy on the floor and back to Sarah. His knees started to give out, so he leaned on the bed. She wanted to buy the bed, he preferred snuggling in their full size, but she insisted they needed more room while she was large and pregnant. He remembered her beautiful face and how much in love they were in the early days of their marriage. Sarah's arm was still bent as though the dinosaur simply hopped out and on to the floor. He sat on the bed feeling defeated. James had it all planned. He would give Sarah the morphine then plunge a needle into his own arm – but now he worried that Sarah, who had not said a word since Joshua's death, was somehow able to throw his toy across the room.

Five Spirits

After retrieving the dinosaur a second time, James sat next to Sarah, kicked off his shoes, and leaned back on the pillows hugging the toy in his arms. The tears came as he laid there silently, confused. After a long pause searching for answers in his head, he again turned to Sarah.

"Sarah if you are still in there can you give me a sign. I don't know what to do anymore. The bills are piling up and I am a mess. I miss Joshua so much and I know you do too. Please say something,.. anything! At this point I would welcome a moan or a jerk. I need you to come out of your darkness. I thought this was the right choice for us. We can all be together again. Just show me a sign, dammit! Will you please show me if you want to live?"

James tossed the dinosaur to the foot of the bed and stood rubbing his eyes turning his back on Sarah. He had been to the meetings, did the research on morphine, and held her hands for months. He glanced back at her as he began to pace. "You left me alone to grieve. He was our son, Sarah! Why do you get to escape into wherever you are and I am left holding down the fort? I planned the funeral, picked out the clothes and chose the casket. I can't do this anymore!"

James went to the bathroom suite to get some water for his cottonmouth and tried to swallow his emotions down like a bad-tasting pill. Resting his hands on the counter top, he stared at his unshaven face in the mirror. Sarah hated facial hair. Without thinking he picked up his razor and smeared the shaving cream. After all, if he was to be found, he should at least look good. He shrugged it off to unfinished business and part of his preparation. Then he remembered he had not left a note. The nurse would let herself in come morning as usual and find their bodies but he wanted to leave a note. James went downstairs and found pen and paper. Sitting down at the kitchen table he tried to find the right words. Both of their parents had passed on, so he paused not knowing who the note was for. "Perhaps it is a confession," he whispered to himself.

"To whom it may concern…" he started, "I, James Arnold, decided on my own that as a husband and wife team, we should end our grief and go to be with our son Joshua…" He stopped, throwing the pen across the room. Smoothing his hair back then wiping his eyes, James stood determined to get the job done. Slamming his hands on the table and kicking the chair he was sitting in across the room, he took a deep breath as he mustered up his courage. Turning off the lights, he stomped up stairs to Sarah's room and sat next to her for one final time. "I can do this Sarah. I will be strong and we will both no longer be in pain. I know you will want the same thing. I love you."

As he sat there with tears making trails down his cheeks, he removed his reading glasses and placed them on the bedside table. James leaned in and kissed Sarah. Her lips were warm as if they were full of life. He loved kissing Sarah. He leaned in and stole another kiss lingering a little longer this time. He smoothed Sarah's hair, marveling at the chestnut color she always claimed to hate. Taking Sarah's hands, he carefully folded them across her chest. "I love you, Sarah," he whispered.

Sitting up on the edge of the bed, James ran a list through his mind. Insurance papers were in order, details for a final resting place near Joshua and Sarah's parents had been purchased, and paperwork placed where their nurse, Willow, would easily find them. All was in place as James took one last glance around the room when he noticed a figure at the end of their king size bed.

"Daddy, don't do it, please!" a small quiet voice whispered.

9~New Normal

After the second meeting ended, the five spirits were left alone once again. Time stood still and had no direct meaning for them. What once felt like hours now felt like only a few seconds. A span, season or phase had little meaning. No alarm clocks for school, no rushing to get dressed, nothing. One minute they were listening to their parents reminisce about happier times and the next it was time for another group meeting.

Pattimore, being the smallest, had retreated to the corner of the room where he was when he first became aware. Harry, who when he was alive was sickly now entertained himself bending, stretching and climbing on chairs beating his chest like the proverbial king of the mountain.

Derek, pretending to hit the highest fly ball in the league, began running bases and waving at the imaginary crowds while Darcy seemed to be fixated with the snack table and the pretty colors. Aaron stood facing the door to the community center, his back to the others. Breaking her trance, Darcy glanced around the room.

"How long have we been here? Does anyone know?" Darcy asked.

Pattimore peeked his head out of the shadow of the corner. "I have no idea how time works when you die, Darcy."

"I know there have been two meetings so far and I think that James person stated there were five meetings. What do you think will happen to us after that?" asked Darcy.

Aaron turned to face the room. "Another three weeks without being able to leave, I suppose. I mean time seems to move fast in a creepy sad kind of way. I don't even know how long I have been staring at this door!" commented Aaron.

Harry jumped down from a chair and scurried to the middle of the room. "I saw a movie once where they all got together in a circle and held hands…then something happened but I forget. Do you want to try it?" asked Harry.

"A game? Count me in!" said Aaron, agreeing.

"It is worth a try, but what is the plan after we make a circle? Pray, say a chant, or what?" replied Darcy.

Pattimore stood and walked toward the group from his place in the corner. "I think that is for séances or witchcraft. We can give it a shot, but can we sit in the circle instead of stand? I am kind of short and it's hard to stand with my arms stretched upward to reach your hands," replied Pattimore. "Comfort is a priority."

"You really are short. Is there a medical reason or just haven't hit a growth spurt yet?" asked Aaron.

"Geez, I thought everyone could tell just by looking at me. I am a little person. Get over it!" snarled Pattimore.

"Okay let's just all sit. Leave the little bowtie-wearing guy alone," said Derek.

Sitting in the circle on the floor each of the five stared blankly at the others until Aaron, rolling his eyes, broke the silence.

"Now is there a plan or are we going to stare at each other?" asked Aaron.

Darcy crossed her legs and got comfortable as she brushed some hair behind her ears. "I used to play a game when I had sleepovers and we called it *20 questions*. It wasn't just twenty, but you get the idea, right? We go around the circle and each person asks a question of the group then take turns answering it. Want to try?" she asked.

"Sleepovers, sitting in circles, bonding and answering silly questions…is this our new life now?" asked Aaron.

Derek chuckled and crossed his legs then stretched his arms in the air. "I would say this is our new normal, we don't have a life. We cannot leave the room, at least not now, and we get to see our parents for five week. Then who knows?" stated Derek.

"Let's just try it!" shouted Harry. "I never got to play any games with other people, never had a friend, or a sleepover. I don't know what lip gloss is either. I want to go first!"

"If we don't let sheltered Harry go first, he will burst into flames," laughed Aaron. "Go for it, Harry! Ask a question."

Harry glanced around the room as all eyes were on him. He put his hand to his chin and tapped his finger as he thought of the perfect question. "Hmmm, I know, what is your favorite thing, toy, or stuffed animal?" asked Harry.

Derek threw his head back and laughed. "It is a strange question but I will answer it. A toy diecast metal race car, I even slept with it. Yep… and it was red. Oh, and my first ball glove. I worked it and oiled it until it was smooth as a baby butt. My two favorite things," chuckled Derek. "Baseball and race cars!"

Leaning forward and getting excited Darcy offered to go next. "I had a kitchen set, dolls, and books but my favorite thing was a karaoke microphone. I loved that the most!" giggled Darcy.

Aaron sat up straight holding his hands in the air. "Okay, don't laugh but I am going to admit while growing up I had a purple dinosaur like the one on television. I slept with that thing every night. I loved that thing. My dad told me I was getting too old for it but I didn't care. I hid it under my pillow. It brought me great comfort. Anytime I was stressed I would hug and squeeze him. May not sound very manly for a man about to enter the army but I admit I was attached," confessed Aaron.

The group laughed at the answers as they sat on the floor in that circle. All eyes turned to Pattimore who was fiddling with his tie as he stared at the floor.

"Pattimore, it is your turn now then I will go last" urged Harry.

Looking up, Pattimore finished adjusting his bowtie and cleared his throat. "I was always the science guy. I loved reading about science, performing science experiments and all that science entailed. However, secretly… I wanted to be a cowboy. One year mom bought me a stuffed horse. It was almost as big as I was, but I was thrilled. A chocolate brown stallion with a blonde mane. It came with its own leather saddle, stirrups, and reins. I named that horse Huckleberry. I had many dreams of riding Huckleberry through a dark forest until I came out on the other side finding a cattle ranch in the clearing. Complete with tumbleweeds, corrals and green pastures. Sometimes I stayed in the forest and became a knight with a lance and armor, then other times I continued on to the ranch and roped cattle in the corral. I watched tons of old western movies. I saw how they threw one leg over the saddle and I knew if I had the chance I would be an expert rider" he paused and closed his eyes. "I loved Huckleberry more than science but I knew I would never be able to ride a horse with my short legs, so I was a scientist by day and a cowboy only in my dreams. I wouldn't want to ever forget my Huckleberry," said Pattimore. He tilted his head toward the sky as if he was remembering his dreams of riding in the sunset.

The group was quiet as Pattimore described his stuffed horse and his deepest desires to be a cowboy. Darcy reached over and gave Pattimore a nice pat on the shoulder. "Pattimore, that was a very touching story. I wish you could have ridden a horse and roped a steer. You have a brilliant mind. We can be anything we want to be in our dreams," said Darcy. "Dreams are the reality we never seem to find in real life"

Harry, having a smile that could not be contained, began rocking side to side in anticipation of his turn to talk. He looked at each person in the circle asking permission with his eyes to speak next.

"Okay, little dude, it is your turn to tell us what was your favorite toy or dream from childhood," said Derek.

Harry adjusted his legs to straighten his back as he prepared to tell his story. "As you know I was allergic to everything, including stuffed animals, so my mother made me a doll made out of socks. The body was from a soft hypoallergenic baby blanket. She sewed buttons for eyes and stitched a mouth and nose. My mom called it my whoobie," said Harry.

"A doll?" asked Derek. "You waited all this time to talk about a doll? Geez, man!"

"Yes, but it was a …um boy doll. Doesn't matter. I loved it and carried it everywhere. It doesn't seem as exciting as riding horses or baseball, but it was my favorite memory," finished Harry.

"Listen, Harry, if it was your favorite then that is all that matters. Everyone is different. A least you had something you were not allergic too. How about another question?" replied Darcy.

"I have one" said Pattimore raising his hand. "What is the one thing you wish you could say to your parent or parents if you could?"

Derek leaned back laying on the floor. "Wow, little dude, that is a deep question. I think we all have regrets. Might worry about the times we disobeyed our parents or snuck out of the house at night to meet a girl, took the car without permission. I mean maybe some of us did that…but personally I don't feel any emotions right now. Not anger, not disappointment or sadness. I just feel peaceful."

"I agree with Derek. I feel no pain, no stiffness, anger, or happiness. Just feel like my worries and regrets have been lifted," replied Aaron. "It is peaceful."

Darcy stretched out her legs and smoothed her dress. "Now that I think about it, I don't feel anything either. I am not worried that I have to go to work or find a sitter. I just feel a warm peaceful sensation, sort of like a hug. That is it, a warm hug."

Harry pulled his knees up and wrapped his arms around them, then began rocking. "I feel great. I feel happy. I have no pain or trouble breathing. Is this what it feels like after we die? No sorrow, no pain, no anger, no worries? Just peace and a warm hug?"

Pattimore nodded his head in agreement. "I think this is what we are supposed to be feeling, so I guess if I wanted to say something to my mom it would be that I am okay. We are all okay."

Darcy lifted a finger to pause the group. "I think I would add to that statement. I would say, *'Hey, Mom and Dad, I am okay.'* Then I would say, *'I am sorry I had to leave you but I am at peace so don't worry about me. I know it is hard and all.'* Or something like that anyway. I am more concerned that my parents will not be okay. They are going to have their hands full now that I am gone."

After thinking for only a brief moment, the group had an almost simultaneous reply.

"Yes, I'm sorry," shouted Harry nodding in agreement.

"I'm sorry I went on the trip." whispered Aaron.

"Ditto" shouted Derek. *"I am sorry I hurt you, Mom"*

"I would say, *'I am okay and I'm sorry, Mom, for blowing up the kitchen.'"* said Pattimore.

The time for the third meeting arrived as though time had hit the fast-forward button. James arrived earlier than usual to make the coffee and carefully lay out the new snacks for the group. Last week, it was sweet donuts so tonight he decided salty pretzels and chips. He carefully opened the bags and poured them in several bowls and placed the napkins in a nice pattern. Everything had to be just right.

"Do you think this guy feels our presence in the room?" Harry asked the group as he moved closer to James.

Harry moved continuously, walking twirling and pretending he had a sword. In his short life he only had small bursts of energy that were always followed by breathing treatments and medications. Bouncing from one side of James to the other, Harry noticed the tablecloth and James carefully arranging the snacks for tonight's meeting.

"Hey everyone, this guy is putting out my favorite snack tonight! I love crunching on pretzels," said Harry. "I could eat them without a reaction, but they made me thirsty"

Darcy walked closer to the snack table. "Sounds nice but they always made me thirsty. However, I would have killed to have one of those donuts from the second night," commented Darcy.

"I am a big fan of cheese and crackers," Pattimore joined in. "It is like a tiny sandwich, only crispy. This dude James put them out the first night and I swear I felt my mouth watering. It was a snack my mom made me while I did experiments in the kitchen"

"I just wish I could eat brownies again. My mom made the best brownies every year for my birthday" Aaron said as he rubbed his tummy.

Derek, who had remained quiet with his hood pulled up over his head, sat up to take notice when the others were talking about food.

"Pizza was my weakness. Ate it all the time," Derek chimed in. "Pepperoni pizza is a food group all by itself!"

James smiled knowing he took pride in choosing and placing the snacks on the table near the coffee and tea. Tonight, he incorporated a few bottles of water to counterbalance the salty snacks. He stepped back and gazed over his display. When everything was set up, he turned to greet the parents entering the room. Some nodded their head in greeting and some even gave a wave. When everyone was settled in their chairs, he closed the door and took his usual position in the middle of the circle to formally address the group.

"The third stage of grief is bargaining. Some say this stage is religious in nature, but not always. In my personal experience, I prayed all the way to the hospital that if God spared my son, I would be a better father, better husband, and better employee. When that didn't happen, I fell back on the anger stage for a while. This, too, is normal processing. We have to go through it.

James swallowed hard choking back his emotions. He lifted his head stretching then cocked his head side to side cracking his neck.

"When my son died, I took my anger out on my wife, Sarah. I regret that because after she shut down, I had no one to talk to and get my feelings out. My friends started to avoid me because all I wanted to talk about was my son's death. I searched for a group. I went through the motions blindly. I never found one group that I felt completely comfortable in. Then I realized it was because we had nothing in common. I did not lose a spouse, an uncle, or a grandparent. Other groups were lumped together. In here, we have common ground," James sighed. "We all lost a child"

Feeling slightly weak in the knees, James decided to take a seat before he went on. Folding his hands in his lap, he struggled to maintain his composure.

"Many of you are thinking, 'then why hash over it again here?' This class is a different approach, and, in the end, you will find peace." He paused, watching the eye rolls and arms folding across the chests as though the parents were shutting down, so he continued.

"In bargaining, we set the parameters of the deal, We set the terms and they are almost always non-negotiable. There is no wiggle room. If we don't get our way, we riot! Does this sound familiar to anyone?" asked James as he casually sat back in his chair.

Five Spirits

"If I know my mom like I think I do, she bargained with God, but I guess the deal wasn't good because here I am," commented Derek kicking his boots.

"We don't know what our parents went through after we…died. I am hearing it, but all it does is make me wish I could still be there for my mom," said Pattimore. "That is why I would say 'I'm sorry.'"

"Ms. Thomas, are you ready to share something about your son, Harry, with us? It can be anger like we shared last week or about bargaining. It is your choice," James encouraged.

Harry's mom sat up straight and stiff like a new pencil, laying her purse in her lap. She slowly rubbed the outside before folding her hands and clearing her throat. She wanted to appear brave and ignore the nausea trying to shut her up.

"I might as well speak and get this over with. I told you all of my fondest memories the first week" stated Ms. Thomas. "Harry liked to put on plays, and they are my most treasured memories. My Harry had talent. I could see it, but I knew he would never live long enough to be an actor, so I let him live his dream even if he became very ill after a performance. The doctors disagreed and thought I should pamper him"

Harry's mother paused and picked up her coffee from the chair next to her and took a few big gulps. "I will go straight to the anger and blame… Harry was always sick. Good days and bad days. I was able to handle most of his care alone, but we also had aides come in twice a week. He had a very bad attack after acting out a scene and the aide called for an ambulance. They said there wasn't much of a chance Harry would make it. The doctor gave him an experimental medicine; it coated Harry's lungs, and he died. His heart failed after his lungs filled with fluid. They worked on him for what seemed like hours and refused to let me in the room. They placed a tube in his throat to help him breathe. It was awful. I blamed the hospital, doctors, and staff. I also blamed myself for agreeing to the new medicine, I just did not want to let my Harry go"

Adjusting herself in the seat and taking the last sip of coffee, she dabbed her eyes and continued. The room was silent as she spoke softly. The pitch in her voice had changed.

"I asked if they could give him some additional oxygen or a new pill to reverse the experimental drug. Please just fix him, I pleaded. They just kept pounding on his chest. I pleaded that if they just let me in the room, if I could just hold his hand then I could maybe bring him back. I talked Harry through many attacks before. Finally, after they stopped trying to save him, I sat by his bed just shouting at the heavens and held his hand," she finished.

The nausea still there in the pit of her stomach, Ms. Thomas turned to her plate of snacks and popped a pretzel in her mouth. "Harry loved pretzels," she said softly, taking a moment to savor the snack her son loved. "Why did you choose pretzels as the snack tonight, James? It is a simple thing really, but it makes me feel like Harry is near me in a strange sort of way."

Five Spirits

Harry Thomas stepped forward with a sad look of disbelief on his face. "I hated going to the hospital. My poor mom. I didn't know how hard it was on her to see me sick," whispered Harry. "She was always so upbeat and loved my plays. Sometimes she laughed so hard she peed her pants. We were best friends. I wish she would have shared that with me. I want her to know I am okay now. *Mom, I'm not sick anymore!*" said Harry.

Swallowing her last pretzel, Ms. Thomas licked the salt off her lips. "If I would have known that he was that sick, I would have let him die at home in my arms and never taken him to the hospital. He suffered because of me allowing that doctor to give him that drug."

Harry moved closer to his mom stopping in front of her. *"No, Mom, do not say that! It is not your fault I was a sick kid. I had a happy life! I do not blame you,"* Harry declared..

"It is okay, Harry," said Darcy as she moved closer and put her hand on Harry's shoulder. "We are all healed now. We just have to hope our parents know that we loved them"

Aaron stepped forward to also stand by Harry on the other side. "I agree with Darcy. Even though we are gone, our parents know we love them. That is the one thing they can hold on to is knowing we love them. Love never dies," Aaron Jackson chimed in.

"Love never dies," repeated Pattimore as he stood up showing support. "Our parents did they best they could."

"I feel the same. Love never dies," repeated Darcy.

One by one the five spirits in the room stood up and went to stand beside their respective parents, even Pattimore. Agreeing that if they had one last chance to show love, it would be in this room, the only way they could.

"I guess my mom did love me and she did not ask for this," said Pattimore. "Besides, I wish I could just tell her it was my entire fault. I mixed the wrong chemicals, but I am okay now."

"From the look on her face, I think she knows, Pattimore. Since the first day I've seen a change in all our parents as they talk," said Darcy. "I think they needed this as much as we all needed to hear it."

Derek pulled his jacket tighter then shoved his hands in the pockets as he stood in front of his mother. Scraping a hand through his hair he raised his head slowly. "I just wish I could tell my mom one more joke and see her laugh. Then I would know she is okay," commented Derek.

Feeling like the entire room was responding well, James allowed the parents to take a small break as they did every meeting. As they headed for the refreshments, James observed the parents chatting with each other as they refreshed their coffee.

"This is indeed progress," he whispered to himself.

Before he called them all back to their seats. He looked around the room at the change starting to show in the parent faces. They were smiling at each other. They were becoming friends in an odd sort of way. He knew that no matter how hard it gets, this class will put it all in perspective. Grief never ends; instead, it morphs into something that attaches itself to your heart and lives there forever. The tug of war with emotions will end and a new, different type of peace of mind will emerge. One they would cling to forever in the acceptance stage.

As the parents who had exchanged looks of understanding and niceties starting straggling back to their seats, James again stood in the middle of the circle and addressed them.

"Does anyone else want to share how they bargained with their child, their spouse, a doctor, or even the heavens?" asked James.

"I bargained for my Pattimore," Mrs. Gilliam said as she cleared her throat. "I guess you can call it that. After the explosion, I ran into the room and I told him to stay with me. I told him that I would buy him a bigger better chemistry set if he would just live. I begged him to live. I thought he would live for me, but he didn't. I am ashamed that I bargained with him about a chemistry set instead of showering his body with hugs and kisses. My last words should have been I love you instead of screaming don't you dare die!" she finished. Tears spilled over her bottom eyelids and ran down her cheeks, leaving trails.

It was Pattimore that moved forward this time. His small stature was obvious as he again pulled as his shirt collar, straightening his bowtie. He appeared to crawl into his mother's lap putting his small hands on her cheeks.

"It is okay, Mother; I knew you loved me. I have an innate sense of observation and even though I gave you a hard time, I knew you were my biggest fan. If I did not show it before I hope you know it now,"

cried Pattimore. Wrapping his ghostly arms around his mother's neck, he buried his face in her chest.

"I think I can still smell the lavender soap my mother bathed in," said Pattimore.

"Do you think we can still smell after we die?" asked Darcy.

"It is not a scientific fact but, in my mind, I can smell her. She always smelled like lavender," replied Pattimore.

James paused to let the room think about bargaining and the consequences. In his own mind he remembered every detail of bargaining with God for his son. After Sarah shut down, he found himself sitting on the bed next to her bargaining again for her to just wake up and yell at him.

Sitting back in his chair, he continued, "When bargaining fails, it leads to guilt. Do not feel guilty for pleading for your child to live. It is normal. We can all agree we loved our children more than the moon; however, I hope you all can grip the fact that they are aware of how much you wanted them to stay, grow up, go to college, or even get married. They know and felt your love. Find some peace in that. If they were here in this room, they would surely feel the love emitting from each and every parent here tonight. Grief is natural, guilt is harmful," finished James.

The rest of the evening was spent listening to each parent talk about how much they loved and bargained for their child. And each child, in spirit, expressed their love in return by hugging their parents. The meeting ended on a good note.

After all the parents filed out saying "good-bye "and "see ya' later" to each other, James turned his attention to the snack table. He was all smiles knowing that the parents were bonding in a way only parents that have survived similar things can do. He had observed Harry's mother exchange phone numbers with Pattimore's. This is the type of wisdom he hoped would develop from his classes: *Teach them to fish and you feed them for a lifetime*. Parents need common friends or any friend to survive and this was the place to find them. All with common goals.

Harry watched as his mother left the meeting, then skipped toward the others who had gathered near the back of the room again.

"I wonder if this dude James knows we are here" said Harry as he jumped up to sit on the snack table.

"He cannot see you, Harry. You are wasting your time," laughed Aaron.

"Maybe if we wave our hands in front of his face, he will feel a breeze and think there are ghosts in the room," commented Derek. "*Boo!*...nah that is just in the movies I guess. He didn't even flinch," he laughed.

"You are all acting crazy. We are dead. Deal with it!" snarled Pattimore.

"We are just fooling around Pattimore, why so grumpy?" asked Darcy as she took a seat beside him.

"I think I am feeling bad that my mother is all alone and living in a shelter. I was never a mushy kid. I was all science and education, shying away from hugs. I regret that now. Now all I can do is hug her with my ghostly arms and hope she feels my presence," replied Pattimore.

"I think my daddy felt my presence when I sat next to him," remarked Darcy. "I am sure your mom feels you are near her too"

"What is the purpose of us being in this room if it isn't for us to see our parents one more time, say special good-byes, feel better about leaving them and for them to feel us in return?" asked Derek.

"That sounds all good Derek, I may feel whole, but at the same time, I feel sad. I think I have regrets or something," said Pattimore.

"I have regrets also, Pattimore. I am supposed to grow older and tell my daughter, Roberta, stories of her grandmother, not the other way around. The five of us need to consider our time here as stolen moments," Darcy said thoughtfully.

"Like a do-over or something?" asked Harry tilting his head to the side.

"Not quite, Harry. More like an opportunity to experience real love before we go away or… umm… disappear or whatever. I mean I think I felt sad but now that I get to see my parents, even if they cannot see me. It makes me happy. Peaceful."

Five Spirits

"I guess you are right, Darcy. I do feel better. I can run around this room and not wheeze one bit. I can hug my mom, do a cartwheel and the best part is I can feel my mother's love. It is hard to explain but I am not sick anymore and that is something to feel positive about. As King Arthur would say, 'you are free now'," said Harry as he danced around the snack table waving his imaginary sword.

Aaron, shaking his head over the conversation going south, stood and walked toward the door. "All I know is when this guy James who is leading the class leaves tonight, I plan to leave. Let's all go stand by the door. I would love to move around outside, feeling peaceful inside. I was always stressed when I was alive. I might see the world in a whole different way."

"I remember feeling stressed. I tried so many things just trying to feel happy again, but nothing worked, then I was hooked and couldn't stop. I am at peace now and I don't want to leave," commented Derek.

"I would only leave here if I could fly. I would fly over the houses of the boys that teased me because of my small legs and drop acorns on the roof. Then they would come running out and I would pelt them with a whole sack of pecans!" chuckled Pattimore.

The other four spirits in the room watched, shaking their heads as as Aaron took his position by the door.

"We must be here for a reason. I want to stay and see my mom and daddy again," commented Darcy. "But have to admit, flying sounds like fun. I would leave if I could fly as well."

"Umm… how do we know if we can fly? Should we stand on a chair and try it?" replied Harry.

Aaron walked back toward the group and stood with his arms crossed. "Listen Harry, we cannot fly, and you should not try it. I just wanted to see if I could leave. That is all. Be cool, little dude. I worry about you"

James continued to perform his nightly ritual of clearing the snack table and wash out the coffee pot. He then changed the tablecloth to orange. It wasn't quite a Halloween orange but more like a football team brilliant orange.

Getting closer to take a look, Aaron felt excited. "Hey, that is my favorite color. I wore a jersey that color when I played ball. I even painted a wall in my room that color orange!" shouted Aaron.

James finished putting away the snacks, saving them for another group, then smiled as he stepped back and admired his table display. Preparing for the next meeting was crucial to his plan. Satisfied, he gathered his coat, walked to the door and turned off the lights. Pausing, he spoke in a low voice "Next meeting I will bring brownies," then he locked the door and left the center

Aaron spun around and clapped his hands looking at the other four. "You all heard that right? He somehow knows I love brownies!" gasped Aaron.

"No way!" shouted Derek.

"I heard it too, we all heard it right?" said Pattimore.

"I have heard, or rather saw it in a movie once that some people can communicate with dead people. Maybe this dude is cleara..clara..voyage…something like that" said Aaron.

"The word is clairvoyant," corrected Pattimore pushing his glasses up on his nose.

"Well, it was in a movie once, so it must be true. What do you think guys? It is possible, right?" asked Aaron.

"What are we supposed to do with this information? I mean, so what if he can hear us. That does not explain how he knows things. He has never spoken to us or had a conversation," Darcy observed.

"Maybe he just loves food, I know I used to love food. I'm sure it is just a big coincidence. Now I am going to try and fly, who is with me?" shouted Harry.

"I swear this dude can see us or hear us or both. Do you remember when he said we were having brownies next meeting?" asked Aaron.

"Yeah, so what is so special about brownies? It doesn't mean anything," said Harry. "Pretzels are the king of snacks!"

"I was standing here when he left, and you heard him say it, right? Then he puts out my favorite color and talks to us!"

"Now that I think about it, he put out my favorite color tablecloth the night he served the donuts. I assumed it was a coincidence" remarked Darcy.

"It wasn't! Don't you all see what I am talking about?" asked Aaron. "There is a pattern here!"

Harry began sword-fighting an imaginary opponent. One hand on his hip and the other waving his sword in the air. He stopped when he noticed Aaron frowning.

"I am not sure I am understanding what you are saying, Aaron. Snacks don't mean this guy can hear us, does it? said Harry.

"Okay, I will prove it. Harry, what are your favorite snacks?" asked Aaron.

"That is easy. Pretzels," said Harry shrugging his shoulders.

"Okay, the night James put out pretzels, what was the color of the tablecloth?"

"Purple! Just like the color of my King Arthur cape!" shouted Harry. "I was the best at swinging my sword. I could have been a famous actor one day. Did you hear my mom say I was talented?"

"Okay, calm down. Not my point. It's not just the snacks…"

Aaron, getting frustrated, looked over at Darcy sitting next to Pattimore. "Darcy, what was your favorite snack when you were alive?" Aaron asked.

"Donuts, although mom told me to watch my weight. She would stop and buy a dozen on her way home," said Darcy. "Why do you ask? I already told you donuts."

"Because I see a pattern. Do you not see it?" asked Aaron.

"I love pretzels, she loves donuts. Who cares?" said Harry.

Harry, feeling like the only one in the crowd who was having fun, decided to sit next to Darcy and Pattimore.

"This feels like a test," said Harry. "I hate tests."

"Oh, my word, it is like talking to a brick wall. You all are way too young to understand!" shouted Aaron.

"Aaron, I think you are getting too stressed. Get to the point, man, no one is following what you are saying, dude," said Derek.

"Pattimore, help me out here. You are the scientist. Is there a pattern here?" asked Aaron.

"Actually, patterns are more a mathematic situation, but I do think I see where this is going. Tell me a little more of your observations,

Aaron, and I will see if I can find a plausible explanation," remarked Pattimore, sitting up to listen.

Throwing his hood back, Derek began to pace in front of the group. Of all five of them, Derek was the most athletically built. He worked out often when playing sports and he had a very manly deep voice. Girls would fawn over him after the games. His self-confidence was always out of this world. When the confidence faded, so did Derek.

"Okay, listen up. Am I the only one who doesn't want to be here? I mean you are all talking about your feelings like babies. Patterns, snacks, colors. What does all this have to do with why we are here?" snarled Derek. "I am more interested in facts like what happens next. Personally, I am a little worried and scared to death about what happens after these five weeks are over and you guys should be too!"

"Whoa, Derek! Man, I am sorry you are upset but we are all dead here, dude. It is not just you," replied Aaron.

"It is just I was so unprepared. I spent my young life preparing for a game or a date. I didn't think things through. I did not expect to be here. We can't change things; we can't go back and change things! What if after listening to our parents go on about how they loved us we simply go '*poof*'?" said Derek.

Derek stopped pacing, threw his hood up, and began to jog like prize fighter in the ring. He began punching the air. He circled the entire room twice then paused at the snack table.

Five Spirits

"Aaron, you asked everyone what their favorite color was and their favorite snack, but you didn't ask me or tell us what yours was. I mean, oddly enough, I think I am catching on to your pattern theory, maybe?" said Derek.

Aaron walked over to the snack table followed by the others. As they all stood there staring at the orange tablecloth, Aaron crossed his arms and proudly stood back.

"Orange, my favorite color is orange!" said Aaron.

"That is so strange because the tablecloth is orange!" said Harry.

"Brilliant observation, Harry" commented Pattimore.

"Hey, you said you weren't going to pick on me anymore, Pattimore. That is not fair. Just because I didn't go to a fancy school doesn't mean I am dumb, you know," replied Harry.

"Again, I am sorry. Seems I am destined to apologize to you everyday, Harry. I open my mouth and sarcasm just spills out like vomit. It is just my personality. Maybe I will hold my breath in the corner until I die," snarled Pattimore rolling his eyes Harry's way.

"What, wait…Oh, I get it," said Harry. "Not funny, Pattimore, because we are already dead…Oh, it was a joke. Never mind,"

"Sometimes you are not the only boat in the moat, ya know. I mean no harm, mainly because you are dead and way too easy to make a joke with. I am having a great time," joked Pattimore.

Aaron, becoming impatient again, took in a big breath. "Listen to me, guys. Every night of the meeting, this James dude places a different tablecloth that is one of our favorite colors. Purple for Harry, Yellow for Darcy, Blue for Pattimore and Orange for me, now do you get it?" asked Aaron.

"I don't get it," said Harry.

"I saw that coming," said Pattimore.

"Pattimore!" shouted Harry.

"Sorry, Harry," said Pattimore as he started to chuckle. "It is just too easy sometimes."

"Okay, settle down. I think I understand and don't worry, Harry, we will explain it all to you, so you understand," said Darcy.

"We just have to speak slowly for him," said Pattimore.

Darcy, getting frustrated, shot Pattimore a side eye, then put her arm around Harry before addressing the group.

"Alright. You are saying that this James person is putting out all our favorite snacks and putting our favorite colors on the table. Got it. But how would he know what we like or what our favorite snack was? He never met us or our parents before, did he?" asked Darcy.

"Maybe we should all think back and see if we can remember him from our past. You know like when we were alive?" said Aaron.

"Maybe he was a coach. Did any of you play ball?" asked Derek.

"Dude, seriously? I never left my house, and I don't think the science boy here had friends," commented Harry.

Pattimore turned to face Harry. Putting a big grin on his face, he reached out, offering to shake Harry's hand.

"That was a good one, Harry. Science Boy, huh? I like it. Now you can give as good as you get. I think we would have been friends if we had ever met. Did you ever play with matchbox cars or any games on the computer?" asked Pattimore.

"I liked to play cards and do magic tricks," replied Harry.

"Close enough. Let's go sit and talk while these guys solve the snack table mystery," said Pattimore.

Derek watched as the two youngest spirits walked away, then turned back to Darcy and Aaron.

"Man, the little dude has a wicked sense of humor but the other one is the type of guy us jocks would have taken behind the bleachers and given him a wedgie," commented Derek.

"Somehow I can picture that, Derek," laughed Aaron. "I wanted to be a jock, but my dad wanted me to join the army. I played a little football but then I changed high schools. I had to make a choice," said Aaron.

Pulling up his sleeve, Aaron flexed his bicep followed by Derek quickly doing the same. Darcy stood there looking at the two shaking her head. She had also been the recipient of bullying. She shifted her weight from one leg to the other, feeling left out of the conversation. The same in life as it was now, no one noticed her. She was present, likeable and she also had a great laugh and smile but always felt invisible.

"If you two are finished comparing your muscles, can we get back to the patterns?" stated Darcy.

"Hey, I would drink energy drinks just so I could work out in the gym and get this way. I think I look good," said Derek still flexing.

Aaron pulled at his shirt to cover his arm and cleared his throat. "Maybe it was just a coincidence. To answer your question, I think we won't know for sure unless brownies appear next meeting, Darcy," said Aaron.

"I think you had a good theory before the muscle show, I was actually catching on. If your hunch is good, then what will be the color for the last week?" asked Darcy rolling her eyes.

"Well, he has put out all our favorite colors except Derek's. What was your favorite color, Derek, and your favorite snack as well?" asked Aaron.

Still continuing to flex, Derek struck a pose and replied. "Red, my favorite football team wore red and I already told you pizza. By the way, Darcy, you know you loved the muscle show, don't deny it!" laughed Derek.

Darcy stomped her foot and clutched her arms to her chest dramatically. "Oh yes, Derek, it was my one desire to see your lovely bountiful muscles…not! Can you be serious for once?" replied Darcy.

Derek pushed up his sleeves, shoulders back, chest out. "I was on the baseball team, football team working out every day. I was even on the wrestling team for a while until I had to wear that tiny onesie leotard. Heck with that. Girls loved me. However, I can be serious when I need to be, but we are dead and I see no reason to think, plan or discuss anything that takes up space in my brain. School is out forever," said Derek.

"Easy dude, you might break something straining that hard," laughed Aaron. "Bring it down a notch or two. I simply said there is a pattern here and I bet the following week the tablecloth will be red. Now let's all cool down and return to the shadows until the next meeting" mocked Aaron.

Darcy turned back toward Derek swooshing her dress as she turned. "By the way, energy drinks are dangerous, Derek."

"Too late with the advice there, Darcy. Too late, indeed. Had I only met you sooner…" Derek snarled.

12~Discussion

The nightly routine changed for James after he contemplated taken his own life and that of Sarah, his wife. Being unprepared and untrained in how to deal with death created a kind of panic response. He was alone without Sarah chatting from the kitchen while making dinner. He missed smelling her clean hair and taking showers together. Everything about Sarah had changed and he hated seeing what the once bright intelligent woman he married turn into a lump of bones on the bed. He hated seeing her so lifeless.

James often thought about their life before Joshua was born. Why was it so hard to go back to that life after he was gone? It would be different, but life was good when they were childless. They were happy then. They went to the theater and patted each other on the bottom when they passed in the hall. But you can't go back.

James understood why it was different for Sarah, as it probably was for all mothers. She gave Joshua life and now there was nothing but an empty hole left in her heart. A part of her was missing and nothing could replace it. After they came home from the hospital, Sarah started losing the thread of conversations, then she barely spoke at all. When she did, it always turned to wailing. It was not like James wanted to forget their son, he just wanted to live without the gut-wrenching pain. It was only when he came to understand that it never goes away is when he gave up. He tried to push through, hoping he would be able to work again or cope one day. He tried.

Sarah, on the other hand, had self loathing immediately. Weight loss, poor hygiene, and dead stares took over her body and mind. James would feel the guilt and anger but still tried to maintain certain routines. He would cry in the shower and pound his chest until it was red as fire. He thought he was normal, just trying to keep the peace. After a week of Sarah laying in the bed, he tried his best to encourage her to eat some soup. It was the day of the funeral and James knew he had to prepare Sarah. She fought his every effort, throwing herself to the floor and refusing to get up.

"I cannot bury my little boy in the ground, James…" was the last words she ever spoke. Sarah curled up on their bed and never spoke again. She withered to mere bones stretched over skin. Her hair grew long and wild. James struggled to brush out the knots sometimes pulling hard to release the tangle but always gave in, letting the wild hair be what it wanted to be. He began to resent Sarah for deserting him.

James's anger turned into a visceral rage the day of the funeral when Sarah refused his help. His nostrils flared. He began punching and kicking anything and everything in the room. He clenched his teeth and shook his fists in the air. All the things that happen after a death kicked in and he lashed out. He pulled Sarah by the hair, trying to force her to stand. Frustrated, he let go of her and she plopped to her side.

Her mouth was open, but no sound came out. James vomited all the anger he had bottled up inside onto his wife that day. He cursed and yelled for over an hour as he paced the room, only glancing at her occasionally. Eventually all the verbal assault came to an end, and he flopped in Sarah's reading chair in the corner of the room. Sarah had given in to her guilt and fell deep into a depression. Something seemed to snap as she lay on the carpet. James, still unsure about Sarah, decided to dress and attend the funeral on his own.

When James returned home, the house was dark. He found Sarah in the same position on the floor as when he left her. Her eyes were fixed and staring at emptiness. She had soiled herself. James called for an ambulance, and they took Sarah away.

Eventually Sarah was transferred to a mental facility to be treated for catatonic stupor. Sarah had succumbed to an inability to move, speak, or respond to stimuli. Her body was rigid and immobile. Doctors encouraged James to visit but he couldn't help but feel jealous that Sarah had somehow escaped the pain and anguish that he was left experiencing by himself. He had a desire to vent and voice his sadness to his wife, but she had somehow left him all alone. Deep down, he knew it was not purposeful, but it felt hopeless and unfair.

As James tried to return to his job, he began feeling fake from wearing two faces. One was strong – as if as if he had it all sorted – and the other was a desire for revenge, self doubt, and loneliness. The only glimmer of hope in his life was Sarah's recovery. Maybe if she got better, they could finally work it out and survive. Even if their life was different, James just wanted her back. Sarah could not engage even at the most minimal level. James was wracked with guilt thinking he had somehow caused Sarah to escape into the darkest pits of her mind even though many psychiatrists explained otherwise. Sarah had underlying mental health issues that came to the surface when she experienced such a major emotional trauma. Her body could not handle it, so her soul retreated. After a year passed, the doctors told James there was no hope. James decided to bring Sarah home and care for her. It was the least he could do.

Neighbors, co-workers, and counselors urged James to try group therapy until, giving in to the pressure, he finally agreed just to make them stop nagging. The first group was a mix of mostly grieving widows with a few others sprinkled in. When they asked him to share, he told them of his son, Joshua. Immediately, he felt the sting of all eyes on him with sympathetic expressions on their faces.

James did not want pity nor anyone feeling sorry for him. He wanted to have a deep discussion about his pain with someone who had also experienced it. He wanted the emptiness, loneliness, and pain to go away or at least bring it to a level he could cope with. He searched for another group, hoping for the best.

In the next group, with the ratio being the same, he decided to slip out quietly during the coffee break. A confident and wise counselor approached him and asked James the question that changed everything.

"What would it take to make you at ease with your son's death?"

"That is an odd question. I don't think anything could put me at ease except to have him back," James snarled.

The counselor stood there holding his hands behind his back and slightly cocking his head to one side. He allowed some time to go by and, assuming he had James's attention, he continued. "Many people want the unattainable answer. Hoping for a miracle or to wake up from the bad dream. That is only in the movies, I am afraid."

"Are you saying there is something that could put me at ease? asked James.

"I am suggesting that you give it some serious thought," said the counselor. "Do you want to find acceptance and peace?"

"Maybe if I could find a time machine and go back to the day he died and change things, do things different," said James.

"That is not possible unless you know where to find a time machine and if you find one, please let me know. We all have a fantasy of going back in time: I had better hair, my wife was still alive, and I would never shout at her about serving the cold peas for dinner the night she had her heart attack," said the counselor.

He let out a small chuckle as he tilted his head back. James did not understand as he struggled to find the right words. He could not understand the question – let alone find an answer.

"I don't mean anything magical or sci-fi. It is a mixed feeling of regret and 'what if' questions that roll around in my head," replied James.

"I understand that, James. It is all part of the stages. At the end of the day, are you asking yourself these rhetorical questions to relieve yourself of guilt? You feel guilty. I feel guilty. We all feel the guilt. We long to be in the final stage of acceptance but fear it means forgetting. It does not. But I ask you again, can you think of any thing that would give you a pass, able to forgive yourself and possibly move forward?"

Getting the impression the counselor was being passive-aggressive to stimulate conversation or to invite a teary breakdown from James, he became red in the face. He felt the vein in his neck start to pulse. He deepened his tone and looked directly in the counselors eyes. "I do feel guilt. I should have been a better parent, better husband, and father! Is that what you want to hear me say?" snapped James.

"Is there such a thing as a perfect parent, James?"

"No I guess not…"

"You cannot go back, and your son can not rise from the dead, so what is left to hope for, James? Can you not think of anything?"

"I…I…guess I hope he is okay. That he is not angry, hungry, or cold. If I just knew he was okay, I could still miss him but have some peace"

"We all want that hope, James, and that is why we come to meetings. There is no right or wrong answer, except maybe that time machine you mentioned. That is a pipe dream."

James repeated those words over and over in his head after leaving the meeting that night. Mourning is a conflict. It is painful and messy. It can force us into corners and prey on our worst fears. It can force us to scrutinize the world around us and never has a conclusion. As James drove home, he tried to imagine a different answer. Of course, if he could snap his fingers, produce a magic wand, or chant a spell over a black kettle of herbs from the garden, then he would most definitely choose to go back in time. He wouldn't argue with Sarah the night before. He wouldn't leave the house without checking the garage, and he would never let Joshua walk alone to the bus stop. As he arrived at home and pulled into the driveway, he understood there was only one answer. There was no magic wand or a time machine. He had to make choices, to take action, and to save what life he had left. The only answer is to know for sure that Joshua was okay.

James rushed in the house and took out some paper and a pen. The old description of mourning, depression and the stages were antiquated. His wife, Sarah, was in a jumbled mess upstairs in her bed, proving lists, medication, and therapy had failed her. He wanted to give in and follow Sarah. He was jealous and angry that she wasn't here facing life at his side. It wasn't fair and he felt hatred rearing its ugly head. *"If love could save us, my family would still be intact,"* James thought to himself.

James scribbled frantically anything that came to mind that may be a better answer to the question he was asked at the meeting: *"What would it take to make you at ease with your son's death?"*

He wrote down many answers, avoiding what he knew to be true. He was testing himself.

"If I had my wife with me and I wasn't alone. Nah, it would be the two of us blubbering and I would have to be the strong one and never let my feelings out. If I had a time machine? Nah that is stupid. If I cried so much that I got over it? Nah, already did that crying. Nope there is no other answer. If I knew he was 'okay' is the only possible answer to this question. But how do I accomplish that?" he said to himself.

James left the paper on the table and methodically climbed the stairs, stopping in Joshua's room. On the bed was the T-Rex staring back at him. As he picked it up, the tears began to form. The room was quiet as well as the entire house. James stared into the eyes of the T-Rex and shook it hard then looked up, closing his eyes. He extended the dinosaur toward the ceiling and screamed. "You were his favorite toy, why can't you tell me if Joshua is at peace!"

13~Depression

The night of the fourth meeting of the special good-bye group meeting for angel parents had finally come. James planned every meeting down to the finest detail so the group could feel how much he cared. Up to now, the parents had become friendly with each other just enough to feel comfortable. The two single parents of Pattimore and Harry had exchanged phone numbers and planned to have lunch together one afternoon.

The group was progressing as planned and James knew tonight was special. He was prepared, dressing in his casual khaki pants and sweater before he went to the kitchen. He carefully followed the recipe preparing the brownies for tonight's meeting and placed the pan in the oven.,

James rubbed his hands together eager for the oven timer to ring. Donning the oven mitts, he leaned forward to take the fresh baked brownies out of the oven and place them on a cooling rack.

"Brownies tonight?"

"Yes, my special recipe. Warm and gooey brownies"

"I wish I could taste them."

"I wish you could too. Do you miss eating?"

"Not really."

"Can you smell them?"

"No, can't smell, either."

"I am sorry about that."

"Its not that bad really. On the bright side, I can't smell when you take an hour pooping in the bathroom, either."

"I don't take that long!"

"Yes, you do…"

With the brownies all sliced into small squares, James arranged them in the container and grabbed his car keys.

"Wish me luck!"

"You got this, Dad!"

Once in the car with the brownies sitting in the passenger seat, James turned onto Highway 301. It was already turning dusk with a few colors still left from the bright orange and red sunset like watercolors across the sky.

Arriving at the community center, James turned on the lights before carrying the brownies to the refreshment table. After taking off his coat, he quickly began arranging the table with small dessert plates, forks, and bottles of water. Next, he rinsed the coffee pot and started the delicious hot beverage brewing so the aroma would soon fill the air. It was comforting when the parents entered the community center, and the aroma of fresh brew filled the air. It was all part of the plan.

Harry's and Pattimore's mothers were the first to enter the room. Both were smiling and laughing as though they were sisters who had just heard a good joke.

"You both look chipper tonight, I take it your week has been good?" asked James.

"Harry's mother, Melanie, picked me up from the shelter for the group meeting tonight so I would not have to take the bus. The weatherman is calling for rain, don't ya know" said Ms. Thomas.

Harry and Pattimore looked pleased at seeing their mothers arrive together. "Hey! Look at those two, science boy! Our mothers are becoming friends!"

"I can see that, Harry, I do have eyes, ya know. Excuse me if I don't stand up and clap," replied Pattimore.

"Hey! Is it time for the meeting again already? What did I miss?" asked Darcy as she joined the other two.

"You didn't miss much. Just Harry's mom taking pity on my mom. That's all," snarled Pattimore.

"Aww… I think that's nice. You two have started getting along and now your mothers are," said Darcy.

"Where are the other two, Aaron and Derek?" asked Harry.

"Time seems to stand still for us, then. On the day of the meetings, we come into focus. Or something magical like that. Anyway, last I saw they were huddled in a corner talking about sports and comparing muscles," commented Darcy.

As Derek and Aaron approached the other three, they all exchanged glances and nods. Darcy, sighing dejectedly, stepped slightly back away from the group.

"Darcy, are you alright? Your shoulders are slumped. Why did you walk away?" asked Aaron.

"I am feeling a little like the odd man out. You know… a little too much mascara and too little confidence," replied Darcy.

"Huh?"

"Never mind," said Darcy

"She is trying to say she is the only girl, but don't worry, Darcy, we still think you are part of the group," said Derek.

"The Dead Kids Group or something like that," said Pattimore.

"It is just that girls will bond over sleepovers or the right shade of lip gloss but boys can buddy up even if they have nothing in common. It gets lonely. I will be glad to see my parents come in tonight," explained Darcy.

Harry looked up at the others from his seat on the floor with his large brown eyes. "I can't feel anything. No pain. No wheezing. Just nothing," commented Harry. "Should I feel something?"

"Again, Harry? We discussed this. We can't feel anything."

As the parents of Darcy, Aaron, and Derek strolled into the community center, the mood in the room turned to one of bonding and friendship. Four meetings with the right choice of people had already improved the demeanor of the group. Change was noticeable in their faces and their physical appearance. They sat taller, casually chatted with each other more and exchanged polite conversation.

"My mom really looks good tonight and I think my daddy is losing some weight. I think they are going to be okay after all," said Darcy, staring at her parents. "I have been so concerned."

"My mom still looks a little angry in the face to me," commented Derek. "I hope she will be okay, I have yet to see her smile."

As everyone was settled down in their seats, James stood in the middle of the room like he did at the beginning of every meeting and addressed the parents. Leaning back on one foot he shoved his hands in his pockets.

"This is our fourth meeting. Five weeks, five stages of grief. The fourth stage of grief is depression. There are degrees of depression, as you may already know," James began.

He paused, swallowing hard, trying not to think of his own depression after Sarah was admitted to the mental hospital. He stood tall, spread his legs in a firm stance and clasped his hands before continuing. "In the moments after denial, anger, and bargaining, we slip into the stage of depression. We tend to pull inward as the sadness and reality grows. We might find ourselves retreating, regretting, being less sociable, and not having an appetite. We reach out less to others, making up excuses. You find yourself laying in bed with no motivation to get up. Ignoring phone calls, choosing isolation," finished James.

As he looked around the room, many parents were nodding their head in agreement. "We want to share again tonight, starting with an instance of how bad your depression was or is now. Of course, you can also add a happy memory of your child to counter-balance. It is not my intention to sour the mood; it is a process. You have to recognize how it happens, why it happens, and when it happens so you can one day look back. Even though it was the hardest test of your life as a human being and parent, there is a way to move out of the cloud of horror and find peace in your memories."

James walked to his seat in the circle. He leaned forward, resting his elbows on his knees, and ran his hand through his hair. "I will start with my experience. My wife never came out of her depression. I would not wish that on anyone. She is in a catatonic state, and I care for her at home. Regret is the emotion of wishing one had made a different decision. Regret can lead to depression, so we have to talk about it. I regretted attacking my wife verbally. It led to my own depression. Depression can sneak up on you or hit you in the face like a raging hurricane. Some people will have dark obsessive thoughts, poor hygiene and eventually get past those symptoms. Some can even become hoarders after a loss. Tonight, we fight the depression cycle by discussing it freely amongst friends."

Pattimore sat rocking on the floor to self-soothe. "My mom may be in the hoarder category. Lord knows, she couldn't throw out a cardboard box to save her life," chuckled Pattimore. "She would claim it was a really good box and she might need it for something someday. Drove me nuts! Not to mention her collection of pointy shoes. Don't get me started!" said Pattimore.

"My daddy has enough fishing tackle to start a museum for old fishermen," laughed Darcy. "What about you, Aaron? Did your mom collect things?"

Flipping his long hair then flashing a grin, Aaron turned toward the others. "My parents collected my trophies, drawings, baseball cards, or anything about me. Seriously, when I wanted to trade them or even throw away the clutter in my room, my mom would flail her arms like she was going to faint. I would get her going sometimes and sit back and laugh until she caught on. Those were fun times."

All five spirits in the room began to laugh, listening to each other's stories and fun memories. Harry was the last to share. His dark curly hair flopped around when he stood up to share with the other four. "One time, I asked the aide to buy me some fake blood. Then I told my mom I had a new acting scene to show her. There I was, pretending to die by the sword like Juliet did with Romeo's dagger. I was so dramatic, staggering and clutching my chest as I pressed the cartridge of fake blood. I thought it was hilarious, but mom almost had a heart attack. After she yelled at me, she began to laugh so hard she rolled on the floor and passed gas. It was the funniest thing I ever heard. We laughed about it for days," said Harry, clutching his chest and pretending to stagger.

James lowered his head hiding a smile, then gained his composure and continued. "Depression is a normal path, we just can't stay there. We deserve to move on and have a life because that is what our children would want. Remember that. It is what our children would want us to do. For us to continue to live"

"Oh, my goodness, that dude said what I was thinking" shouted Derek. "The thing I hate the most about all this is seeing my mom look so sad."

"I think we all agree on that one, Derek," Pattimore chimed in.

"Let's all go sit by our parents again. I think when they feel our presence, they can't be sad anymore," said Darcy.

"Good idea, Darcy. We have to let them feel our love so they know we are still here in sprit and will always love them," echoed Harry as he and the others ran to sit next to their special parent.

James paused to allow his last words to sink in. He saw shoulders drawing up, arms pinning across the stomach as each parent thought back to their depressive behavior. Mrs. Tenner raised her hand cautiously like a shy school girl.

"Yes, Mrs. Tenner, do you have something to share?"

"I was just wondering if anyone else in this group saved things that belonged to their child, and do you think that is hoarding?"

There was a slight chuckle that spread around the room. "No, I don't think that is hoarding. I personally still have all my sons' dinosaurs. I did eventually donate most of his clothes, though. Does anyone else want to talk about their depression stage tonight?"

Mr. Williams, Darcy's father, raised his head then sat back in his chair. "I have something to share. It is not hoarding dinosaurs or anything, but I got really down for a while. Didn't think I was ever going to find an interest in anything. I kept the fishing rod she used. My wife packed up most of her things and donated them. We cried all the time. No matter how hard I tried to keep it under control, I would burst out in tears. It is a tough thing for us men to be strong and hold it in. When we started coming here, I felt Darcy was with me and telling me to keep fishing," said Mr. Williams. "My Darcy was the apple of my eye. It has been very hard, but I think there just might be a light at the end of the tunnel. I started eating better, got on the vegan train, and I am slowly feeling better"

"Thank you for sharing, Mr. Williams. Sometimes it takes a change such as a new job or even a diet to assist us in finding our way out of depression. Men can cry too. Anyone else want to share before we take a break. I brought brownies tonight! I baked them myself."

Aaron's mother sat up straight when she heard the announcement about brownies. "Oh, my Aaron loved brownies! I haven't made them since he left us. I lost my desire to do most anything if it reminds me of him. I suppose I am stuck in that depression stage. My husband seems to be doing better than me," commented Aaron's mother.

"Mr. Jackson, would you like to respond to that?" asked James.

Mr. Jackson leaned back in his chair crossing his arms firmly. "I am military. I learned to see horrible things, then put on a brave soldier face. I am not happy with that, but it is in my training"

Five Spirits

Aaron's mother rolled her eyes and bit her lip before lashing out at her husband. "Military or not, I have not even seen you cry for our son! I feel you don't care!"

"I don't think this is the place to discuss that dear," stated Mr. Jackson sternly.

"If not here, then where? If I start to speak about our son, you leave the room. I need to cry, I need to talk about him. Why are you so stiff?" cried Mrs. Jackson. "This is the cause of my depression: no one to share it with!" said Aaron's mother.

Mr. Jackson dropped his chin to his chest. He took a few long cleansing breaths then looked up at James. He felt the room close in as all eyes were upon him.

"I am sorry for the outburst. I know my wife is hurting and I do not blame her. I saw so many dead bodies in the military. I joined during the end of Vietnam. I was shipped over immediately after swearing in. I was only nineteen. We married the night before I shipped out in her parent's back yard. I came back a different man. If I am to keep my cool, I have to block things out. I am unsure what I am supposed to do, how to act, or how to comfort my wife. She won't eat, can't sleep. I hate to leave her and go to work. This group is our last hope."

James nodded. "Everything you said is normal. Your background, the way you were raised and even your DNA make up who you are, how your react and even how you will respond to situations in life. There is no rehearsal for the right words or actions when it comes to dealing with a sudden death. If you scream, it is your normal. If you cry, that is your normal coming out. If you curl up on your son's bed and whimper like a baby hugging his favorite dinosaur…still normal. You were handpicked for this special group, Mr. Jackson, as well as every parent in this room, and I promise you that you can and will find peace. I am not saying you will be perfect or back to normal, but you will find peace."

James continued, "However, one thing for certain: it is extremely hard to find that peace if you do not let what is bottled up inside of you come out. Talk to your wife, talk to this group like you just did. Share the good times and the bad times. Share you guilt, your anger and the way you have handled it so far. Share how you are not sleeping, share how you started to call your child and got three numbers dialed before you realized you cannot call them any more. No judgment, no regrets, not here. We all have felt like you are describing."

Mr. Jackson nodded in agreement, then quite unexpectedly snatched a tissue from the box. He buried his head in his hands and began to sob openly. His wife moved closer and placed an arm around his broad shoulders. The two of them sobbed together. They came together as one for the first time since Aaron's death.

Aaron stepped closer to his parents and leaning forward he blanketed them with his ghostly body. Tissues could be heard being ripped from their boxes as the entire group felt the moment. A shared feeling of loss as well as a shared feeling of letting go.

Five Spirits

Darcy stepped forward and waving a hand at the group of five spirits she approached Aaron and put her hand on his back showing support. Slowly, one by one, the five spirits gathered around Aaron and his parents. Piling up, embracing, and gathering as best they could, hoping the parents of Aaron would feel their presence and comfort.

Recognizing the Jacksons were having a breakthrough, James sat silently for a few moments. Darcy's parents began hugging each other then stood up to join Aaron's parents. Harry's mother scooted closer to Pattimore's mom and Derek's mother grabbed a fresh box of tissues for the group. After a few loving, crying moments, James stood up and clapped his hands. "Who wants brownies?"

After a few short minutes, Aaron's parents joined the other parents at the refreshment table.

"Look, you guys! My mom is eating the brownies!" said Aaron pointing toward the refreshment table.

"Isn't this part of that pattern thing you were talking about Aaron? I mean the color of the tablecloth and your special snack?" asked Pattimore.

"Yes, Pattimore, but who cares right now? My mom is finally smiling. I think she is going to be alright. My passing was hard on her. She thinks I ran away but I didn't. At least I wasn't running away from her. I was just running," said Aaron

"What was that all about Aaron?" asked Darcy.

Aaron pulled at his collar and starting scratching mindlessly at his ears. "I enlisted in the army like my dad. I was leaving for boot camp in two weeks, so a few of my buddies I met at enlistment wanted to take a road trip. My dad said no, that I needed to workout to build my strength before leaving. It is stupid, I know, but I just wanted some fun before I left home" said Aaron.

"Right on! A party before the crew cut regimen. I can understand that totally!" commented Derek.

"It wasn't exactly supposed to be a party, more just a road trip and a few beers. We ended up in the mountains and one of the guys dared me to climb a rock formation. I slipped and fell, wedged myself between two boulders and couldn't get out. Crushed my lungs. The other guys were drinking and didn't realize I was missing until it was too late. My last thoughts were of my parents. I should have never taken the dare. Shouldn't have had those beers either. Made me think I was invincible and bulletproof," said Aaron.

"I understand that courage you feel from alcohol. My mom thought she was the cool mom allowing me to have a few beers with her when I was a young teen. One thing always leads to another. I thought drinking was cool. But hey! Your mom is eating brownies. That is a sign she is going to be alright," said Derek.

"Just like that James dude said, we want them to keep living," Harry agreed.

"Yes, the only thing I want right now is to know my mom will be alright and frankly, I think this James dude knows how to help with that. I mean, I don't know how he knows but he is putting out our favorite snacks, our favorite colors and getting them to talk. I think he is a helpful guy," said Aaron.

"We have been trying to find a way to help our parents feel our presence and ironically this James person is doing it with food," said Pattimore. "It is brilliant!"

James was listening to the incredible changes as the parents were chatting while enjoying the brownies and having a warm cup of coffee. Harry's and Pattimore's moms were hitting it off so well it pleased him immensely. There was some talk of moving in together. That would get Pattimore's mother out of the women's shelter and a companion. Even Aaron's father was out of his seat and enjoying the refreshments. He was usually the one who stayed seated during the break time. His back rigid, his eyes focused with no expression.

James noticed the plate of brownies diminishing as everyone snacked and shared stories. Everyone's expression was different than the first night they walked into the community center. Once again, he found his way to the center of the circle and waited for the parents to quiet down before he began to speak.

"As we continue to talk about depression brought on by a sudden tragic death we must remember and believe in the fact that there is a light at the end of the depression tunnel. I didn't care if there was a light at the end, I just wanted out of that tunnel. We may think it will never happen. That we will never be happy again. We dig our feet in and refuse to smile because that would be wrong to be happy. It is guilt. Guilt leads to depression, and depression takes us down the tunnel," stated James.

James shoved his hands in his pockets and casually looked at the low pile carpet on the floor of the community center. He remembered when guilt reared its ugly head. Guilt is what took his wife Sarah down the path of depression.

Pattimore leaned forward with his elbows on his knees, listening intently. "I can understand my mom having that concern. If she allows herself to laugh or smile, then it means she has forgotten me."

"That is not true Pattimore. I want my mom to be okay enough to smile, laugh or enjoy a good meal without the guilt" said Darcy.

"I agree," said Harry. "Moms are people, too, and my mom deserves to laugh again or eat all the cheese she wants. It doesn't mean she don't love me anymore."

Derek lowering his gaze began staring down at his feet. "I understand guilt all too well. I felt guilty for what I did but I don't want my mother to feel that way. There has to be a way to let her know she can move on and enjoy her life somehow," replied Derek. "It is not good for our parents to stop living."

After a long pause, James walked to the refreshment table and gathered some pens and paper he had brought for tonight's meeting and began to pass them out before he stood again in the middle of the circle and addressed the parents.

"Every parent goes through the stages, starting with denial, and we cannot deny that. Sorry… bad joke… We quickly move to anger as we have discussed, then bargaining until we reach depression. What happens in this stage is what creates the path for the rest of our lives. Some get stuck, some get in a holding pattern for longer than necessary because of guilt, and some push through too fast. No matter what stage you are in, you can find a way out and here is why…Your children would want you too."

James shuffled over to a seat in the circle ,hoping to not appear as a leader but one of the parents. He, too, had lost a child and it was his wish to simply share some skills and not become a cheerleader for angel parents. Leaning back, he crossed one leg over the other and held up his pen and paper.

"Who is up for a little project and some homework?" asked James.

"Oh, boy! Nothing like being back in school," laughed Derek.

"I sure miss school. At least I think I do. Can you have a few feelings if you are dead?" asked Pattimore.

"You are the scientist, Pattimore. You tell us. I never attended school," said Harry.

"I think you are just remembering school, Pattimore. I can remember my daughter. Her face, her curly hair just like mine. Fishing with my daddy. We still have our memories, I suppose," commented Darcy.

"I remember teasing my little brother. I would put him in a headlock and give him a knuckle noogie till he cried. It was all in fun, but he would pout until I gave him one of my toys to keep him from telling my dad. Fun times," laughed Aaron. "I think yes, we do remember things."

Derek threw off his hood and stood in front of the group. His body posture was that of a batter at home plate. He raised an eyebrow and curled his lip, placing his leg out and pretending to kick the dirt off of home plate. "I still have the best memories. Bases loaded and I am up to bat. The crowd is chanting my name, Derek! Derek! The pitcher throws the first ball. It is a foul, I step aside so it doesn't hit me and toss the pitcher a look. He throws the next pitch and I make contact with the ball, hearing the crack of the bat! It is a fly ball way out over the second basemen's head. I throw the bat down and take off running… first base… second base… I am rounding third and heading for home when the outfielder throws to the pitcher. There isn't time to throw it to the catcher, so he runs to tag me. My foot stomps down on home plate and I am safe! We won the game with that run," says Derek. "Yes, we still remember."

"Wow! You must have been a star player! I watched baseball with my dad. We watched football too," replied Darcy.

"You are tall. Why didn't you play basketball?" asked Pattimore.

"I am not that tall, just taller than you, little dude. Basketball players have to be taller than me, but in baseball you can be any size and still be as good if not better than anyone else," replied Derek.

Tilting his head to the side and looking up at Derek. "Maybe I could have played baseball if I hadn't exploded our kitchen," sighed Pattimore. Then laughing he grinned. "Nah… Too short for sports."

"I guess that proves our memories are still intact," said Darcy.

"That seems to be the one constant for all of us. We have our good memories. No anger. No pain. Just good thoughts," agreed Pattimore.

Pattimore sat on the floor, criss-crossed his legs, and began rocking slightly with his arms crossed. "Uh… This project thing James mentioned could be scary. My mother admitted she cannot read. I hope he doesn't plan on embarrassing her," said Pattimore.

"I am sure this James guy knows what he is doing, Pattimore, let's just watch and listen," said Darcy. "Maybe it is a game of some sort. If we have our memories of them, they have memories of us and that will help them to be okay."

The parents were talking among themselves wondering what the project was going to be as they gobbled down the last crumbs of brownies. Pattimore's mother, showing signs of wariness, began rubbing her forehead. James took her concern into consideration as he began to explain the purpose of the project.

"The good news is no one is going to see what you put on this paper unless you want to share it. Let us start with guilt. Everyone feels as though they should have done something different and therefore they dwell on that until it turns into a big heaping plate of guilty stew. You continue to load your plate until you can't possibly eat all that is served, and your stomach begins to hurt. What is in your stew?" paused James as he glanced around the room.

Aaron stepped away from the others and rushed to sit by his mother's side. "I know my mother feels it was her fault that I left. She is most likely choking on her guilty stew. I think I will just sit right here beside her giving her my good vibes," said Aaron.

"That is a good idea, Aaron, let's all go sit by our parents in the empty seats beside them and just maybe they will feel our presence again. This is going to be a tough one to get through," chimed in Derek.

As the five spirits scooted into the empty chairs beside their parents each one placed an arm around them in support. Every other chair was a spirit sitting next to a parent. Derek sat back nonchalantly and threw a leg over his mothers lap. Aaron took his seat next to his mother, pushed back his hoodie, and put his head on her shoulder.

"I can't decide which side to sit on. Both of my parents need me tonight," commented Darcy. "I will just scoot in between them."

Pattimore, swinging his little legs, smiled over at Darcy. "Stand behind them and put your arms around both of them! We can do this, guys. Let's show our parents support!t" cheered Pattimore. "Hurry, Harry! Come sit by your mom like me."

James shook his head both in disbelief and wonder as he leaned forward in his chair. "I left empty chairs between each set of parents for a reason," James said softly.

Harry paused as he passed James to get to his mother. "He knows we are here. I swear he does. He looked right at me!" shouted Harry as he placed his arm through his mothers and held her tight.

James looked down at his paper again and continued. "What you write on your paper is for your eyes only. Now let's continue. A stew contains meat and vegetables such as carrots and potatoes. The meat is you and your relationship with your child. The heart of the stew. Let's say the potatoes are your guilt. Big starchy gummy, stick to your ribs guilt. The carrots are the floating docks of hope. They all mix together in the stew, but they are also separate. Draw a circle on your paper. Your child's name is the meat, the potatoes are the things that make you feel guilt, and the carrots are docks you could grab a hold of to pull your self to the side and out of the stew. Keep it simple" instructed James. "It seems simple, but it will make you aware of how you are bogged down."

"Mom was a great cook. She made the best stew I ever ate," claimed Derek licking his lips. "That gravy… man, it was good!"

"I am confused," said Harry.

"It is an analogy, not real stew," groaned Pattimore.

"Okay, science boy, I think we get it," said Aaron.

After James made some sketches on his paper, he held it up to show the other parents.

"It may seem silly, but I think making it simple helps us see that it is only as hard as you make it. My child's name was Joshua. The heart of my life, part of my stew. The stew represents my family unit with all its parts. Sarah and I were the gravy that held everything together. We added the potatoes of guilt, blaming each other for not watching over

Joshua. The stew got thicker. The carrots were there to support us, an additive to the stew to make it all better. Our family, neighbors, clergy, doctors and even therapist – but we pushed the carrots aside. We pushed everyone away. What is a stew without the carrots?"

James continued his soliloquy. "Our life brings the good and the bad together in the gravy. No one has a perfect world and there are no perfect parents. There is definitely no perfect pot of stew. Sometimes it is too salty, or the meat is undercooked or tough. It happened. A child died. So I ask you this: What would it take for you to find peace with the way the stew turned out? What would it take for you to stop feeling guilty over the death of your child?" asked James.

As the parents sat looking at their papers, James gave them time to digest his analogy. They slowly began to draw and scribble.

"I am still confused," commented Harry.

"Listen, Harry, sometimes things in our lives look like a pot of stew. All mixed up, it is one pot of stew, but it took a lot of ingredients to make that one pot, or something like that," replied Darcy. "Don't think about it too much."

"I don't like carrots," replied Harry, poking out his bottom lip.

"It is not about the carrots, Harry. Just listen."

James decided to stand again and walk to the middle of the circle. "Now let's talk about how to get past the guilt. Get past the depression and eliminate the sticky, gooey guilt. Does anyone have any suggestions?" asked James.

Darcy's mother raised her hand to speak as she sat up straight in her chair.

"Yes, Mrs. Williams, please share whatever you like."

"Please call me Nan. I felt guilty about a conversation I had with my daughter before her accident. Maybe I could have been nicer or said anything that might have prevented the accident. Darcy had so much on her mind that day. Those thoughts are my sticky guilt and it pops up in my mind every day. How do I make my mind stop?"

"That is a good example of guilt, Mrs. Williams. It is normal to feel the guilt, explore the what if's and examine every minute of behavior before the accident. Don't get lost in it. I mean, could you look back a week, month, or year and know for sure that what you said to back then were not something that caused the accident and not the few words you said that day?" James paused. "I don't think there is a way to narrow down the actual words that made a difference. Those are the things that we need to let go. Instead of wondering if you were to say different word,s let's focus on the positive words and strengths. Think more about all the good conversations you had with your daughter. How many conversations or words did you say to your daughter in her lifetime?"

"Millions and billions I suppose," chuckled Mrs. Williams.

"A few words that day did not cause the accident when you compare it to all the millions of positive words you spoke to her over a lifetime while being her mom," James stated.

"I never thought of it that way. We did have some really good mother-daughter talks," said Darcy's mom.

"Of course, you did. You talked to your daughter from the day of conception. Those positive things are the sunrise and sunset. The few negative words that fall in between are all erased when the sun goes down. Those brilliant colors as the sun sizzles in the horizon means it is done, the day is gone and forgotten. Every day is a new day and the day before is just a memory"

The room became quiet. Mrs. Williams grabbed a tissue and buried her head in her hands. There was not a dry eye in the room. The sound of tissues being ripped from the boxes could be heard, followed by gentle sobs. Again James stood in the circle, giving a cleansing pause before he spoke once more.

"As parents, we have to rely on the love and guidance we gave our children for however many years we had with them. A few cross words are just a part of life. I guarantee your child is not thinking about that now. If they can remember anything in their next life, it will be the good times and all the love you had for them. We get depressed from the guilt, so we take to our beds. We cry or scream. However, if your child were to be in this room right now, listening to you all talk about your guilt, they would be worried that you might not move on. Take an appropriate amount of time to explore that guilty depression then focus on the good memories. Focus on your strengths. Focus on all the good and bring those positive memories to the front and cherish them. There is a litany of ways to convert your thinking of guilt to thinking of the brilliance they brought to your lives. Perhaps spend time in nature, watch a sunset…"

"My daddy went fishing!" Darcy interrupted, breaking the silence among the five spirits.

"Shhhhhh, Darcy! This guy is good," scolded Derek.

James began to slowly walk around the circle of chairs. "Go fishing, take a hike, and go to a dog park. You have to get that Vitamin D and sunshine to combat the depression," agreed James.

"Didn't I just say that?" asked Darcy. "I think he heard me!"

"Yes, Darcy, we heard you. Fishing, Fishing, Fishing. Now will you please let him continue?" replied Pattimore.

Derek's mother put her hand to her chest, her eyes prickling with tears. "I felt that guilt from words I said, and the depression tried to pull me in after my son died. Everyone says they are afraid of dying, but once you lose a child, I am now afraid of living. Life has lost its meaning. I went back to work. I looked at old photos. I purposely pushed myself to remember the good years. I listened to his favorite country songs. At first, nothing worked. I joined a few groups, but it didn't feel comfortable. My daughter asked me to do something spontaneous. We went camping." said Derek's mom.

"That is on the list of how to fight the depression, Mrs. Tenner. Listen to music and do something spontaneous. It is reprogramming your brain to stop dwelling on the death. Did it help you feel better after camping?"

"I think it did. At least while we were sitting by the fire, dancing to silly music and swatting mosquitoes, my mind made new memories to push some of the bad to the back of the filing cabinet in my brain. All that is just temporary, though."

James continued, expanding on Mrs. Tenner's thought. "Everything is temporary. You fill your cup with iced tea and it is full until you drink it. Your grocery cart is full until you take it home and put it away. Your gas tank is full until you use it up. They key is not to fill your cup then forget about it. You have to fill it up again and again until your thirst is quenched. Your heart and mind are filled with good memories of your children. Don't let the tank run dry. Do what it takes to keep it full!"

James announced another short break while he pulled out a chalk board on wheels. He knew this sounded like high school, but he remembered how he finally found peace and wanted to share it with his group. The end of their sessions was getting nearer.

Darcy stood up, massaging her temples while she joined the other spirits during the break. "They have to get better! I hate seeing my parents upset. Do you think that is what this group is all about?" asked Darcy, watching her mother blow her nose.

"I think they are getting better, Darcy. I have seen a change in my parents since the first meeting when we all realized we were dead," replied Aaron. "They smile, then they cry. They hug, then they argue but at least they are talking."

Harry strolled across the room, frowning. "Why is this dude James pulling out a chalkboard?" asked Harry. "I had a small one at home but the chalk dust made my lungs wheeze, so my mom threw it away. I got it for Christmas one year."

A wide grin appeared on Aaron's face. "Don't get me started on Christmas memories! My favorite time of year. I was spoiled when it came to presents. Those little metal cars, I had hundreds. I got video games out the wahzoo!" laughed Aaron.

Pattimore did a small jig in place, moving his little legs and swinging his arms. "I admit I am discontent with the way things presently are, being dead and all. However, my mind is replaying past events, especially Christmas," said Pattimore. "Mom always made a huge ham, sweet potatoes, and cornbread dressing. Most of my memories have to do with food. I love ham."

Harry, standing in the group, suddenly became quiet exchanging secret glances with the others as they reminisced. "You all seem to have amazing memories of Christmas. I think we may have been too poor to have a big fancy dinner at Christmas time, but I did get a few presents. One time I got a coloring book and another time I got a magic set!" exclaimed Harry.

The other four looked at Harry with uncertainty in their eyes. Darcy stepped forward and pulled him close, hugging him tight.

"What? I loved to color. What did I say wrong?"asked Harry.

"You didn't say anything wrong, little dude. Come here and give me a hug, too!" replied Aaron.

"Can I get in on this hugging thing?" asked Derek. "Talking about Christmas makes me happy."

"Group hug!" shouted Pattimore. "Hey! Watch out! I am short, remember? Someone lift me up. I want to be in the group hug too, don't ya know!" said Pattimore raising his hands in the air.

Derek hoisted Pattimore up and the group hugged. Laughing and giggling ensued until they fell into a heap on the floor of the community center. The parents in the room totally oblivious of the warm memories being passed around by the spirits of their children in the very same room.

Sprawled out on the floor of the community center, Pattimore made an imaginary snow angel. "Look, guys, we can do what we want and no one can see us. I used to love the snow at Christmas. How about you Harry?"

"No, I couldn't get cold by playing in the snow, Pattimore."

"Did you live in an apartment like me and my mother, Harry?"

Harry, looking sheepish, leaned back on his elbows. "Well, I said I think we were poor because we didn't have elaborate meals, but we did have a big house," said Harry.

Assuming the others would be angry with him, Harry stared at his shoes and banged them together. "It doesn't matter anyway; I was not allowed upstairs and we had plastic covering the windows so no dust would come in the house and make me sick. I guess it was like an apartment."

The other four glanced at each other then back at Harry. Derek was the first to grin and the smile was infectious.

"Listen, it doesn't matter, Harry. We understand," said Derek. "We all lived different lives when we were alive. Its all gravy."

Darcy glanced over at the snack table then sat up, smoothing her dress. "Let's go see what James is talking about now that our parents consumed all the brownies," said Darcy.

Five Spirits

"Yeah, I want to know what he meant by homework," replied Pattimore. "Call me strange, but I loved homework."

"That is strange, Pattimore," replied Derek.

James positioned the chalkboard to one side of the room so all the parents could see. As the parents took their seats, James began writing a list of ways to fight depression. He then turned to the parents and folded his hands in front of him. "Depression is a struggle between opposing emotions over what you want to do, have done or plan to do. I am not telling anyone to avoid depression stages, I just ask that you incorporate some of the things listed here in your life. You may have to force yourself and you may just say no to a few things. Just keep it in the back of your mind that one day you will get past the depression. I am obligated to share this list with you:

1 Find a way to experience nature even if it is in your own backyard. Look at the tall oaks standing with firm roots.

2 Do something spontaneous, like go to lunch with a friend.

3 Read a book that will take your mind to a new setting

4 Focus on your strengths and the good memories

5 Take a long, hot bath

6 Listen to music while dancing

7 Clean your closet or organize your junk drawer, let your mind drift away and wander."

As James wrote the list on the chalkboard, some parents were nodding and agreeing. Others were shaking their head. When he finished, he placed the chalk back in the tray below the chalkboard. James let the parents absorb his short list while he began to pace again. "I have gone rags to riches and riches to rags. I fought hard and I have also given up. Yes, I also felt like giving up. That should not surprise anyone. Holidays are the hardest, followed by birthdays. I say celebrate those days. Lay a wreath at their grave or write a letter to your child. Many go through the five stages of grief and get stuck in the fourth stage, depression. I think it is clear, you cannot stay there. You cannot live there. Find a way out so you can move and live on. Your children want you to. There is a sunrise and sunset every day and they are free, try to see more of them."

Pausing only for a moment remembering the last sunset they watched as a family during the only vacation they took before their terrible loss. James cleared his throat and pushed on.

"Personally, the final stage called acceptance was the hardest for me. I was so afraid to go there because in my mind I thought it meant forgetting. It does not mean forgetting!"

James allowed more time for his words to sink in. Taking his seat again in the circle he leaned back and folded his arms. In remembering his own depression and fear, he understood what might have been going on in their minds and it was his desire to help. Recalling the conversation he had with the leader of the last group he visited, he was sure this group would find the peace like he did.

"Are there any questions before we finish for the night? I did mention we have homework, right?" he chuckled.

Parents sat up in their chairs, anticipating what James meant by homework, and glanced around the room at each other. Pattimore's mother sat back and began rubbing her chin. Recognizing that as a sign of uncertainty James encouraged her to share with the group.

"It is okay to be worried, concerned, or scared. Emotions are normal. What is on your mind, Mrs. Gilliam?" asked James.

"I don't mind admitting I am scared of the last stage. You say its not forgetting but I am *not* sure I can accept anything about the death of my child. I still have things I can't shake off. It will take more than a spontaneous trip or a hot bath. It is hard when you don't have the atmosphere needed for recovery. I feel so depressed living in that shelter after losing my apartment. I really just want to go to sleep and never wake up," said Mrs. Gilliam.

Pattimore stood and wrangled his body onto a chair to be taller. "Mom, no! You have to live on!" shouted Pattimore.

Harry, worried about his friend stood on a chair next to him. "Your mom came to the meetings, Pattimore. She is not going to give up. I just know it. My mom lives all alone in that big house, maybe she will ask your mom to come stay with her, Pattimore" said Harry. They seem to have become friends and that is what friends do, right?"

Pattimore and Harry both climbed down from their chairs and ran to sit beside their mothers as the others stood watching, their mouths gaping as Mrs. Gilliam continued talking to James.

James sat forward in his chair and clasped his hands together resting his elbows on his knees He wanted to choose his words carefully: contemplating death was a normal reaction after a sudden loss of a child, and he understood that better than anyone. "I was in the same head space as you are, Mrs. Gilliam. I didn't want to live on without my son and my wife. I understand what you are saying, and I applaud your bravery for opening up to the group. Living on after we bury our child seems unnatural. Remember what I said earlier. Our children want us to live on. Not be miserable, sad, and depressed, but live on," said James. "If Pattimore was in this room listening, he would tell you to continue to live your best life. If that best life is in a trailer, apartment or even a shelter, please just live on!"

Pattimore's mother took a tissue to cover her face. Her mouth opened like she was about to scream but no sound came out. She tried to compose herself, her cheeks flushed. "I am sitting here, doing what you say, and listening to what you say but I don't feel a change. I still miss my Pattimore and I am all alone. There is only one more meeting left and I find myself uneasy. I can't help having a sensation of desperation right now. I have loved meeting the other parents and I am especially grateful for Harry's mom giving me a ride but what do I do when these meetings end?" asked Mrs. Gilliam. "I feel all alone."

Five Spirits

In a gentle tone, James began to console Pattimore's mother. "I understand your uncertainty but let's not let it bleed into other decisions and situations. You have not been able to complete all five stages of grief yet and I am here to guide you through. Do not be afraid. Basically, you feel stuck and I understand that more than you know. You as well as everyone in this room were handpicked for this five-week group because of your unique situation. You *have* made progress. You made a new friend with Harry's mother and all of us here in this room will remember you always. It is completely normal to have doubt. You will feel change. You are not alone, Mrs. Gilliam."

"Why do I feel so alone and definitely not normal at all? I feel crazy – like I am the only one not better!" shouted Pattimore's mom.

James stood up, closing his eyes briefly. "I am not watching at a distance and hoping for change. I am right here with you. I will help you. You are not crazy, weird, or abnormal. None of you in this room are abnormal. No one here is all alone. We have each other now. Please remember that. The sole purpose is to help you heal, live on, and feel peace. In the end it will all make sense. You will not move on blindly, but instead have people with like minds be your comfort. Please trust in yourself a little longer"

Pattimore started pacing, his little legs working hard to carry him. "My mom is not okay. What can we do?" asked Pattimore. "Who has a plan? Where is Harry?"

Looking over at Harry, they noticed him on his knees appearing to whisper in his mother's ear. On his knees in the chair his hands cupped near his mouth like a megaphone.

"Harry, our parents cannot hear us. What are you doing?" asked Aaron curiously. "We need to stick together and find out how to make our parents be okay!"

Winking Harry looked briefly at the other four. "I am planting a seed, as my mother would say, and hoping it grows."

Throwing his hands in the air, "Wow! Plant a seed. Make a list. Life is just not that simple," remarked Derek. "There is only one more meeting and our parents are still struggling while we sit around and chat about Christmas. This is not good."

"What are you trying to say, Derek?" asked Pattimore. "At least Harry is trying."

"Listen, I am all for trying. I had a great early childhood. I played ball, went to races, talked to girls, but I still messed up. Do you think that if I made a list of things to not try or mistakes to avoid it would have saved me? Let us keep it real" replied Derek as he began to pace.

Darcy stepping forward and looked at the other four, her hands on her modest hips. Harry jumped off his chair near his mother and walked over to the group as Darcy started to speak.

"Listen, I think I understand. Things are usually great until they are not. I loved to sing. I sang all over the house, starting at age two. My parents were my biggest fans. I thought I would be a singer one day and pictured myself up on stage with crowds cheering. We had a nice house, we went fishing. I had pets and a nice room. But I still messed up. It was me who didn't listen to my parent's advice. Instead, I listened to a boy. No lists or putting me in the corner was ever going to change my mind," said Darcy. "My parents tried. They were loving parents but one day I decided only I knew what was best for me. It happens sometime around age twelve. However, I was wrong, and I should have listened."

"Get to the point, Darcy!" shouted Aaron.

Darcy clenched her teeth before continuing. "The day I ran into the truck, it was a gray, windy day. The kind of day where you could smell the rain coming. I loved the smell of rain. I had the radio on and was singing along to the top of my lungs. All I could think about was how the father of my child was possibly going to jail so I was singing, trying to get my mind off of it. Don't think my parents didn't warn me, made a list of people to stay away from, lectured me, and even threatened to disown me! They tried everything. I thought I was smarter. I could handle anything. I was a grown up. Ha! I was no more a grown up than the man in the moon. I kept thinking I could fix it. I was in love. I imagined in my messed up thinking my parents were trying to keep me from being happy, like they had chocolate and were hiding it under the bed to keep me from it."

"That all sounds normal teenage stuff, Darcy. What is the point, please?" mumbled Aaron, putting his hands on top of his head.

Darcy paused and, looking down, she shuffled her feet swaying from side to side. "I guess I am trying to say, my mind should have been on my safety and the road with the upcoming rain. It was an accident. Not my parents' fault. I don't care why it happened. All I can care about now is that my parents will be okay without me. The time for blame and anger has passed. We need to focus on finding a way to help our parents move on. If that takes a list or Harry trying to whisper in his mother's ear, then so be it!"

"I think I understand what the feisty Darcy is saying. I loved football and my parents got to see me play for only a few short years. So… they had good times then but they feel cheated now. Cheated from seeing me grow up. Now they are struggling because their dreams for me did not come true. I wasn't a football star and I never made Sergeant in the Army. Unfinished business. Wishes that won't come true. So this James dude seems to know what he is doing. Make a list, lecture them, or allow them to crumble in their chairs and cry it out. Let's all calm down and hope he can help them, right?" said Aaron. "That is what we want."

Harry put his arm around Pattimore. "We have to let this play out until the final act, my friend. We all want our parents to live on and have peace like the James dude says. His list might help. My whispering in mom's ear might help. We got to try."

Derek placed the palms of his hands together and stood in front of the group motioning for them to gather around. "I still say this James dude, as you call him, can hear us or even see us. He knows things about us," chimed in Derek. "There are no other plausible explanations for all the coincidences between what we like, our favorite color or even what we are talking about. He can make all the lists in the world but all we can do is hope it works. He also lost a child. I wonder why he isn't here with us."

"Maybe we should search the room. I haven't explored all the corners. Maybe he is hiding?" replied Harry.

Rolling his eyes, Aaron turned to face Harry and Pattimore still with their arms around each other. "We don't need to search for anyone. We need to find a way to show our parents we are okay, so they need to be okay. Am I right?"

"I want my mother to be okay, that's all," replied Pattimore.

"I think we all agree," said Harry.

"We all agree," said Darcy.

"So, I think it is safe to say we all agree, but how do we do that?" asked Derek. "We can't go out and buy them flowers or anything."

"My mother loved pink and white carnations. They last longer than roses do," said Darcy. "She would say a handful of wildflowers are pretty too. Such a good mom. I hope she knows I loved her even when I was rebelling over something silly."

"Okay, then that is settled. No flowers," joked Derek.

Harry wrinkled his nose, rubbing it hard. "Flowers make me sneeze."

Aaron looked up and closed his eyes. "It is sad, Harry, that you never got to smell the lovely sweet fragrance of a stargazer lily or the perfect red rose. It is an aroma that can fill a room."

Five Spirits

Harry's mother stood and sat next to Pattimore's mother and began rubbing her back. The other parents expressed kind words and encouragement to Mrs. Gilliam. James allowed some time while the other parents comforted Pattimore's mother. This is the exact response that was needed, and he was proud of the way the parents rallied around each other. Soon parents of Aaron, Derek, and Darcy all took a minute to offer tissues and water to Pattimore's mother, comforting her and patting her shoulder. The group was coming together and supporting one another. After an acceptable amount of time passed, he knew he had to bring the meeting to a close. Everyone went back to their seat drying their eyes, emptying most of the tissue boxes James had placed around the room.

Placing an arm around young Pattimore's shoulder, Darcy gave a comforting side hug. "I am glad my parents have each other. I can only imagine if my mom was alone, or my daddy for that matter, when I died. It must be harder on single parents like your mom, Pattimore. It was hard on my parents. I can feel it. I was born on Christmas Eve, so now it is hard for them to celebrate the holidays, too. We would have my favorite meal and I would get to open birthday presents. Always wrapped in birthday paper to make me feel special. Don't worry too much. It's okay for your mom to cry and it's also okay to have a laugh. Your mom needs a friend. It doesn't mean she is forgetting you."

Five Spirits

"I was her whole world. Now I wish she had made friends, but we couldn't afford a babysitter for me. We were the poor family, unlike any of you," said Pattimore.

"Friends are important to get through the tough times, I suppose," replied Darcy. "Let's not focus on the past."

Derek leaned back in his chair and stretched out his legs. "My mom was a single parent when I died but she had a ton of friends and quite a few she called best friends. It is true you need friends to get by. I lost most of my friends because of my behavior," whispered Derek. "I am pleased she came to this group."

James stood in the circle again and cleared his throat. "I like to say we are all friends in common. We may not have ever met if not for these meetings, but we will remember it always. Now let me explain that homework."

James chuckled at the groans in the room. "Now, now…This is not like any other homework you ever had. Trust me. It has two parts that, in the end, will come together and make sense. For he first part, I want you to write down an answer to this very important question…" James paused, noticing the grimace on Pattimore's mother's face.

"I will need help with that, I can't write too good," commented Pattimore's mom. "Pattimore helped me write notes and stuff."

Pattimore rolled his eyes. "Oh, and she is back to the embarrassing stuff. Geez, Mom! One minute she is crying and the next, out comes the pity talking. But she is my mom, I love her."

"Hush, Pattimore, I want to hear this!" Aaron interjected.

James took a short walk around the circle to collect his thoughts before continuing. "Here is the question that I was asked by a brilliant counselor. It changed my life. Please believe me that the answer to this question will also change your life." He paused for effect.

Slowly and emphatically, James continued, "What would it take for you to be at peace with your child's death and accept it?"

James stood silent looking at each parent in the face, making eye contact. "Think about that and we will address it next week. Think hard. There is an answer. You may say nothing in this world will ever make me be at peace but there is an answer. Remember, you are not forgetting, just accepting that you cannot change the facts. But… What would it take for you to be at peace?"

While letting the parents have a moment to think about his question, James walked over to his bag near the refreshment table and pulled something out. Turning with confidence and a smile James walked back into the circle of the room and held up his son's favorite dinosaur: the Tyrannosaurus Rex.

"This is my son's favorite dino. He loved the T-rex more than any other toy. He slept with it since he was one year old. He brought it on trips and even took it to school for show-n-tell" he paused.

"When I hold it, I can still smell him…"

"When I hug it, I feel his presence…"

Five Spirits

James emphasized each sentence and held the dinosaur up for all to see. "At our last meeting next week, I want each of you to bring in any item that was something of your child's. Not just a picture but something they loved, touched, and cherished. Their prized possession. It is very important to choose the right item. It can be a stuffed toy, a football, or even a toy soldier. It only matters that it was special to them for most of their life or at the end of their life. Something physical. Something you can hold in your hand. Now you have your homework, let's all go home. I look forward to our last group session. It will change your lives, as it did mine." The words flowed from James's tongue as if they were a prayer.

Watching as each parent gathered their belongings and started to shuffle out, James noticed Harry's mother hanging back to talk to Pattimore's mom. He stepped closer, listening to their conversation without being obvious. He was still hugging the T-rex as he pulled a chair closer to the two women.

Harry's mom slapped her hands on her thighs loudly. "It is settled, then. I need help removing the plastic and taking care of that big old house and you need a home. Besides, I get lonely without my Harry. I miss his smooth olive skin and his black curly hair and lordy, he had the biggest brown eyes! I wish you could have met him. He had a laugh that was contagious. I often wondered what he would have become if he wasn't allergic to everything and so sickly. The world lost a good one when we lost my Harry" She nodded toward James, then looked back at Pattimore's mother. "Truthfully, I have been so lost and lonely that I considered selling the house now that his laughter and smile has left. I was meant to come to this group so I could meet you, Ruth Gilliam, as well as James here. Let's get you out of that shelter and into a home where you belong! I will pick you up tomorrow," said Harry's mom. "You can call me Melanie. We are going to be roommates!"

Wiping her eyes, Pattimore's mother looked over at Harry's mom and began to smile. "I suppose if it is no bother. I am so alone without my Pattimore. I would love to have someone to talk to when my feelings attack me and thoughts swell up in my throat. We could share a meal or a cup of tea, and I am still capable of pushing a broom. We will have that place cleaned up in no time!" said Pattimore's mom.

James stepped a little closer to the women. "Did I just hear that you two beautiful women are going to be roommates?" asked James.

"Yes. The thought just came to me tonight somehow, as if I was nudged," replied Harry's mom. "I don't know why I didn't think about it before! I have been rambling around in that big old Victorian house feeling sorry for myself. I even began talking to myself. Lord knows, the neighbors probably think I am having a breakdown. Now, it is time to start living! I am going to do something spontaneous, James. You should be proud. I am starting with removing all that medical equipment from my living room! Next, we can take down the plastic from the windows and, who knows, we might paint the walls a bright yellow," replied Harry's mother.

Five Spirits

Nodding his head with a big grin on his face, James stood facing the woman. "It sounds like a good project for you two. Busy hands can be a blessing. Think of grief as a maze made of hedges and being lost in it is more than okay. Be spontaneous, dive in, and challenge each other while keeping company!" commented James.

"It was a house I inherited from my parents. Harry and I lived mostly downstairs because of his illness and being allergic to everything in the world outside. I had workers come in and wrap the inside windows in plastic. He was kept in a healthy bubble environment, complete with air purifiers. In the end, I guess it all was a waste of time. The doctors didn't know what else to do for him. I haven't touched anything since his passing. It is time to clean it all up and I guess I have you to thank for it James. You and your list have inspired me," said Harry's mother.

"Don't forget to bring something of your son's to the next meeting. We will be serving pizza as well," replied James.

As the two women turned to leave, James walked over to the refreshment table to start cleaning up. He placed his son's T-rex on the table and began to brush the crumbs off the orange tablecloth. Having the T-rex with him and watching it stare back with its blank dark pearl button eyes, gave him comfort. He remembered buying it for his son after a visit to dinosaur world. Joshua cried and begged even though it was a bit pricey, his wife Sarah convinced him to buy it. James claimed that this dinosaur phase would pass, and they would have wasted money. However, Joshua carried that dino everywhere and slept with it every night. James looked at the T-rex and nodded. *"Money well spent,"* he whispered.

After all the parents left, the five in the room slowly gathered near the refreshment table to watch James. Derek walked to the other side of James and stood there with his arms crossed and a smug look on his face.

"Anyone want to take bets on what color the tablecloth will be for the next meeting?" asked Derek.

Pattimore tapped Derek on the leg to get his attention. "I am very curious now that you and Aaron have clued us in to the patterns, Derek" said Pattimore. "Science always wins."

"Let me lift you up onto the table so you can see better, little dude!" replied Derek.

"I don't want to be in the way," whispered Pattimore.

Aaron stepped behind Pattimore and assisted Derek in lifting him up. Grabbing him under the arms, they plopped Pattimore toward the end of the table. Pattimore proudly adjusted his bowtie as he sat high on the table. At the same time, James was removing the orange tablecloth.

Flabbergasted, Pattimore squealed. "He took it off with me sitting here! Did you see that?" he shouted. "It went right through me!"

Five Spirits

Harry laughed as he stood on his tip toes straining to watch. Aaron and Derek nodded toward each other and together they scooped up Harry and sat him right next to Pattimore.

"I want in on this. I am hopping up on the table too. Come on! Let's all sit on the refreshment table!" shouted Darcy.

Aaron and Derek looked at each other and shrugged their shoulders. Simultaneously, they both hopped up on the refreshment table awaiting a reaction of some sort.

"We might as well have some fun with this James dude," laughed Aaron.

"Yeah, I can't wait to see him try and put on the next week's tablecloth with us five sitting here," replied Derek.

"We must look like Mount Rushmore sitting in a line. No dead presidents, but still, we are dead just the same," Pattimore snickered.

Aaron crossed his arms and sat up straight. "I guess we are about to find out if this James dude can see us or not. Surely, if he can, he won't be able to put the new table cloth on. Challenge accepted!"

Harry, being the actor that he thought he was, started making faces and crossing his eyes. "Let's all make a scary or silly face when he comes back from cleaning out the coffee pot. Maybe it will scare him," said Harry.

"He is a nice guy. Maybe we shouldn't haunt him or scare him away. We need him to make sure our parents are alright," commented Darcy.

Derek tilted his head to look at Darcy. "No clutching your pearls now. We started something as a team we finish as a team!"

"I think this is funny, I never had a team. Heck, I never had any friends until all of you," said Harry, waving his arm in an arc towards each of the others.

Pattimore, in his usual sarcasm, commented. "There is no team in science, except maybe in a competition to see who discovers the first vaccine or cure for cancer. Nope. I was a solo chemist. I was working alone the night I blew up the kitchen. Not fun at all. Not impressed with my work, no do-overs either."

"It is good that you can joke about it," said Harry.

"It is not a joke, Harry. I literally blew up the kitchen. Haven't you been listening?"

James finished with the coffee pot and put it away, ready for the next meeting. He stood in front of the refreshment table and put his hands on his hips. After a moment, with an odd grin on his face he reached in his bag to pull out the tablecloth and turned his back. In one smooth motion, James turned, flipping the tablecloth like a bull rider swirling his cape in the air. The tablecloth snapped open and then like the sail of a boat, he let it gently float down onto the table. "There. It's all set. Next week this red tablecloth will be the right setting for our last meeting," he said aloud. James picked up the T-Rex from the table and headed for the door. Pausing to turn out the lights, James turned back toward the five still perched on the table. "Oh… and it is also going to be pizza night."

James loved to tease the spirits. Sometimes he felt guilty not telling them from the beginning that he could sense their presence in the room, even see them. It was better to leave a small sign or comment as he left for the evening. Time meant nothing to the spirits. In between group meetings the concept of time vanished. He did not understand it; he just knew that they could not experience loneliness, pain or worry so he was satisfied the experience was not harmful and left it at that. Never sure if their future was strolling through fields of flowers or singing with the angel's choir, he was sure that it would bring them unimaginable joy.

Aaron jumped off the refreshment table with such vigor he nearly knocked off young Harry. "Did you all hear that?"

Derek, right behind him, jumped down and did a pretend football spike in the endzone, then proceeded to do a little dance like he had just made the touchdown of the century. "I sure did! Look at that red tablecloth…my favorite color! And we all heard him say pizza night…my favorite food! It is proof! Don't you all see it?"

Darcy slid off the table with a concerned look on her face. "I heard it, but what do you think it means? We still cannot leave this room." she said.

"Okay. Hold up. Before we get too excited, this tablecloth doesn't prove anything," chimed in Pattimore. "We need more evidence. Does anyone recognize this place we are stuck in?"

Derek jumped off the table and held out his arms as he looked around. "This building? Yeah it has been around since I can remember. We had scout meetings here and in that corner over there, I kissed Shelly Monroe after a sweet sixteen dance. She had blonde hair and blue eyes. She was wearing a blue sleeveless satin dress. It was my first kiss," said Derek.

"Ewww… You kissed a girl?" said Harry.

Putting his hands on his hips, Derek gave Harry a stare. "Yes I did, little dude, and if you would have grown up then you would have most likely kissed a girl as well. It was thrilling. I remember it well." replied Derek.

"Okay, enough about your love life, Derek. Why do you ask if we recognize this place, Pattimore?" said Aaron.

"Curiously and suspiciously, this room is familiar to me as well. My mother brought me here for a science group when I was six. Can it be we all know this building and this room? Maybe that is the connection?" said Pattimore.

Darcy stepped forward, doing a small dance twirl. "I took dance lessons here. I knew I recognized this old place. What do you think it means?" asked Darcy.

Aaron, who had been standing with his arms crossed listening to the others, finally spoke up. "Hold on… If this place is where I think it is…I played county football right outside those windows on the south. I remember a field with just a few trees at the far end and a pond. My old neighborhood is just beyond that where we rode bikes until the streetlights came on. This just gets stranger and stranger," he said.

The four of them looked over at Harry. "Don't look at me!" said Harry. "I never left my house, at least I don't remember leaving the house except to go to the hospital. I have no memories here," said Harry.

Darcy approached the table to assist Pattimore to get down then offered help to Harry. "I am fine for now. I like being as tall as everyone else even if for a little while," said Harry.

Pattimore placed his hands on his hips and looked up at Harry still perched on the table. "Harry is right. Help me back up. I like talking eye to eye" he laughed. "Being able to look people in the eye instead of the crotch is something to experience when you get the chance," laughed Pattimore

As Darcy and Aaron lifted Pattimore to sit on the table, Derek joined them. He scratched his head as he thought. "Harry, are you sure you don't know this place? There is a small playground with swings on the other side of the building. Maybe you played there when you were younger?" asked Derek.

Harry straightened his back and crossed his arms thinking hard. "Another thing I have never done. Swings! Bet that is shocking. This is becoming some kind of game show where we guess all the things Harry never did in life. Geez, you guys! Thanks!" said Harry. "Besides, there are many other things we could have in common besides swings or this creepy old community center."

Aaron raised his eyebrows looking at the others hoping he was not the only one trying to muffle a laugh. "Nah, Harry, we just thought you might have forgotten or something. Seriously, though, you never got pushed on a swing so high you fell out? It is a right of passage! He laughed.

"No. I never got on a swing, climbed a tree, played in the snow, or kissed a girl like Derek said he did. I guess I am the boring one in the group," said Harry. "But that is okay, I can run faster than anyone!"

Five Spirits

Pattimore clapped his hands together. "Let's have a race! I put my money on Harry!" he said, trying to swallow his laughter.

Derek shook his head and turned away to hide his grin. Turning back to the other four he said "Let's leave the little dude alone."

Darcy moved closer to stand by Harry. "I can empathize with you, Harry. Me being a girl, I wasn't allowed to go to many places unless I had someone with me. That can be a bummer."

Pattimore leaned toward Darcy. "You do know that is not the same thing, right? Harry couldn't leave his house because he would get sick, not because he had strict parents. It's like your empathy took a left turn," snarled Pattimore.

Darcy crossed her arms then turning abruptly she stomped away shouting over her shoulder "I was just trying to help!"

The four boys watched in silence as Darcy disappeared from their sight to sit in the dark corner of the room. The corner that she first appeared from on that first day of the group meetings. Harry and Pattimore still sat calmly on the refreshment table as Derek and Aaron exchanged glances.

Harry, feeling particularly devious, whispered to Derek, "Now that she is gone, can you tell us a little more about your first kiss, Derek? I want details!" said Harry breaking the silence.

"Like what do you want to know?"

Harry shrugged his shoulders "I dunno. Were you nervous? Were her lips soft?" asked Harry. "I watched movies."

Pattimore leaned in, listening. "You can tell us, Derek. There is no chance we will ever tell anyone. We are dead, remember?"

Aaron took a hand and slapped his brow. "Geez, didn't you dudes get the birds and the bees talk?"

"I studied bees, they have a stinger. It is science" replied Pattimore pressing his lips tight defiantly.

Derek threw his head back cackling. "You are killing me. Not actual birds and bees but you know the talk that your parents give you when you…ummm…never mind…"

Pattimore and Harry exchanged looks of disbelief, then shrugged it off. Aaron covered his mouth hiding a slight laugh, then let out with a slight giggle. Shortly afterwards, he grabbed his stomach and let out a full gut-wrenching laugh leaning his head back like a rooster crowing at the sunrise. The laughter was contagious and the four of them slowly began to chuckle until Harry snorted. Clamping his hand over his mouth his eyes bulged out. This started another wave of laughter. Pattimore laughed so hard that he almost lost his balance and fell off the table. Harry grabbed the back of his shirt to pull him back. All the commotion made Darcy curious, so she stepped out of the shadows and stood with her hands on her hips, staring at the boys.

"What are you guys laughing about? What is so funny?" demanded Darcy. "Are you talking about me?"

The boys fell mysteriously quiet as they all turned to stare at Darcy, trying hard to maintain their composure. Pattimore cleared his throat and straightened his bowtie. In a calm clear serious voice, he said, "We were discussing the science of bees and their stingers."

"Pattimore!" shouted Derek. "You never tell, dude. Geez!"

Darcy's mouth gaped open. Pointing at Aaron and Derek, she began to mumble. "Were you..ummm were you two trying to explain…oh never mind. This is unbelievable. Boys can be so gross!" said Darcy. She stood with one foot slightly in front of the other, pursing her lips angrily.

The sight of Darcy being angry set off another round of belly laughs. Soon Darcy caught the laughing bug and joined in, not being able to resist. She pressed a hand over her mouth trying to stop herself. After a few minutes and a slight pause, Harry looked at the others very calmly. "I am so confused right now…but I actually don't care!"

Slapping Harry on the back Pattimore laughed. "This is the most fun I ever had talking about bees!"

"I have never even seen a bee except in a book," replied Harry.

"Allergies?"

"You betcha! Mom said if I ever got stung by a bee, I would swell up like a balloon. It sounds fun but I never wanted to find out," said Harry.

Derek, Aaron, and Darcy could not contain their cackling as they listened to Harry and Pattimore talk about real bees. Soon Derek was throwing high fives with Darcy and Aaron, then slapping his knees as he bent over roaring with laughter. The joyous, uncontrollable laughter filled the community center. They couldn't even look at each other without another giggle escaping no matter how hard they tried. Aaron pinched his nose and held his breath trying to contain the chortle.

Worn out from laughing, Darcy took a seat in the center of the chairs and propped back on her elbows looking up at the ceiling. Derek and Aaron assisted Harry and Pattimore off the refreshment table and casually wandered to the circle to join Darcy.

Aaron plopped down and folded his legs underneath himself. "Listen, it has been great to laugh. It has been great to see my parents and it has been great to meet all of you. If we weren't dead, we could be friends possibly. But we know we only have one more meeting and the group sessions will be over for our parents"

Harry, resting his head in his hands leaning forward with elbows on his knees, became very quiet. Derek spread his legs and stretched to touch his toes as if he was exercising before a big game. Quiet had replaced the laughter.

Darcy sat up crossing her outstretched legs and began brushing imaginary crumbs from her dress, avoiding eye contact with the others. "I always wished I had a big house on a hill with lavender and rosemary growing in a box on the window sill," she murmured wistfully.

Pattimore adjusted his glasses and tugged at his bowtie before speaking. "What do you think will happen to us?" asked Pattimore quietly.

Five Spirits

Darcy looked up at the five of them sitting on the floor. "I know we can't take anything with us but we can leave something behind," she muttered.

"What is that, Darcy?" asked Aaron.

"Love. We leave love behind," replied Darcy. "That is what 'Life After Death' means. You give so much of yourself to the people you love while you are alive that so much remains behind. What survives is not our body, but love. Love survives."

Every night after the group meeting,s James followed the same routine. On his way home, he drove slowly by the school his son attended. He took his time so he wouldn't get home too early and have to sit and hear the dreaded report from the nurse how his wife was not improving. He turned the car toward home, driving slowly so he would pull into the driveway at exactly nine o'clock. Just when the nurse's five-hour shift ended. The nurse arrived at four p.m. on the dot every Wednesday (unless she ran into traffic) and they agreed to a five hour shift only. This gave James time to leave the house, grab a coffee, and get to the community center early to prepare.

Nurse Willow was the same age as his wife Sarah and agreed to work the same shift every week so a new nurse would not have to be trained to care for Sarah. James appreciated the dedication but hated having conversations. Many times, he detected a bit of flirtation but had no trouble ignoring the subtle hints that she was single and ready to mingle.

His weekly routine was to walk in the front door dragging his feet and looking down at the floor so the nurse with the first name of Willow would assume he was too exhausted or depressed to exchange idle banter. James was not interested in chatting it up with someone named after a tree. His wife Sarah was the only woman he would ever love. As soon as he mumbled some vague good-byes and closed the door, he would set down his case and go through the house turning out the lights. Willow insisted the light was good to cure depression, but James liked the dark and hoped to keep the electricity bill at a controllable level. He started in the living room, turning out the two lamps next to the leather couch Sarah insisted they needed, then next to the dining room and den before heading upstairs. He and Sarah looked at several houses with a Realtor before deciding on this one with the hardwood floors Sarah loved so much. James complained that the house was too big for a young married couple, but Sarah disagreed.

"I am going to raise all our children in this house, James" Sarah would say with a pouty lip. Not able to resist the pouty lip, James gave in and put in an offer for the house. James surprised Sarah, taking her out to their favorite sushi restaurant. He made arrangements ahead of time and when the waiter sat them at the table, the key to the house was wrapped neatly in a box on her plate. Sarah squealed with delight as she planted kisses all over James's face. They were now homeowners with a mortgage.

Sarah, at the time seven months pregnant, picked out curtains and wallpaper the next day and insisted that all upgrades had to be done, as well as the nursery, before their first child was born. James and Sarah spent every weekend until the early morning hours, eating take out and painting walls. When Sarah went into labor the nursery was decorated in bright colored dinosaur wallpaper with matching curtains. Seeing Sarah so happy made it all worth the effort.

When they brought Joshua home from the hospital, it was the happiest day of their lives. Soon with the night feedings they were sleepless shadows passing in the night. Sarah stayed home with Joshua for six months before going back to work. She had lost most of her baby weight and was proud of herself when she looked in the mirror. They both agreed they needed the income but worried about Joshua going to daycare so they decided on a nanny until Joshua could start pre-school.

The first years with Joshua turned out to be an adventure. Joshua was a charmer with big brown eyes and soft curls in his hair. His eyelashes were naturally long, and he would bat his eyes and melt your heart. They never wanted to cut his hair until strangers started telling them, "What a pretty girl they had." James insisted he take Joshua for his first haircut and Sarah cried the whole time, scooping up a few curls to put in his baby book.

Joshua grew tall at an early age, taking after James's side of the family, but never lost his charming attitude. He used his charms and killer smile to get an extra cookie from Sarah or a second dessert at a restaurant. Teachers described him as a good and helpful student, always volunteering to help another child struggling with their math. It came as no shock that the morning of his death he would take matters into his own hands, walking himself to school. That was the way Joshua was: never causing any trouble.

Five Spirits

As James sauntered in the house after the fourth meeting at the community center, doing his usual shuffling of feet, Willow stood directly in his path. Willow stood there with her coat on, hands on her hips, staring up at James.

"Please, I am especially tired tonight, Willow. Can we save the small talk for another night, perhaps?" asked James.

"You do look tired, James, but you said that same excuse the last time I was here. In fact, you say that every time. I could take a full-time position at the hospital if I didn't enjoy seeing your sour puss and working here so much. We have to talk about Sarah's condition and the fact that you are not eating right or I will have no choice but to refer you to an agency to find another nurse to take my place," she replied.

Willow hoped the fear of finding a replacement would force James to agree to at least talk to her. She was fond of Sarah and James, too. She tried to keep her emotions professional but seeing James so down all the time made her feel something she knew was not right. It didn't take a nursing degree to notice James avoided her and she hoped it was because he felt something for her as well. The diagnosis for someone with Sarah's condition was not promising and James would eventually be all alone.

"It is not your job to worry about me, Willow. If you insist, then I will allow you just ten minutes to give me a report on Sarah – then I must ask you to go home so I can rest. Do we have a deal?"

"We only have a deal if you sit at the table eating the food I prepared for you while I talk and you listen, Mister Grumpy-pants!" she replied with a not-too-subtle twinkle in her eye.

James sighed, knowing he had to agree or waste time arguing, so he put down his satchel and hung up his coat. He stepped to the side of the foyer and glanced up the stairs. He didn't know what he expected to see but lingering downstairs with Willow made him out of sorts. Nothing and no one was there, so he shrugged his shoulders and entered the kitchen. When he entered the dining room, Willow had already removed her coat and was seated with her notebook at the ready. A huge bowl of steaming hot beef stew was pushed in front of James.

"It does smell good. Seriously, this is not necessary, Willow. I usually grab a sandwich or something. I never asked you to prepare a meal for me," said James as he dipped his spoon in the stew.

"I am glad you like it, James."

Pushing the bowl back slightly, James put his hands in his lap and lowered his head recalling a memory. "I just remembered the time Sarah burnt the breakfast eggs, so she tossed them in the trash with such fury one slipped behind the bin. We walked around for days wondering where the smell was coming from. Sarah swore she would never try cooking again," James laughed. He then became silent again and slowly looked up meeting Willow's gaze from across the table.

"It is okay to talk about Sarah around me, James. She is and forever will be a part of both of our lives," replied Willow.

Five Spirits

James reacted with an immediate apology. Willow reached her hand across the table and gently laid it on James's hand. He stared down at it for a moment then slowly pulled it away, sliding his hands back into his lap.

"I just can't, Willow," James said, shaking his head. "I know it has been over two years, but Sarah is right upstairs and I feel as though she is not completely gone. She is still alive and still here with me. I don't expect you to understand," said James, sighing.

Willow stood up and took a seat in a chair closer to James. Reaching out, she gave a slight tug to his chin and forced him to face her. "I understand more than you think I do, James. I have heard you talking to her as though she was your best friend. I get it. Also, just so you know, I also noticed morphine loaded in two syringes a few months ago. Don't worry. I am not going to make a report on it, but I want you to know that I understand," said Willow.

Suddenly becoming aware that Willow's true intentions were not flirtations but concern, James sat up rigid in his chair and reached out to take Willow's hand. "I …I..don't know what to say, I mean I was in a dark place but I don't feel that way anymore. Please believe me. I would never, I mean I could never do whatever it is you think I was going to do. I love Sarah."

"I believe what you are saying but your demeanor and the way you avoid discussing her care tells me something else, James. I am concerned as a health professional. I am the one who is responsible. I should report it. They may have to place Sarah in a safe environment. It might be in her and your best interest"

"No, please. I will talk to you. I could not tolerate Sarah being put in an institution again. I want her here with me. Please… I will eat your cooking and talk your arm off if that is what it takes but don't do anything rash. I am begging you, Willow"

James had mistakenly assumed Willow was looking for a romantic connection. However, it turned out that basically she was concerned for his well being, protecting her job and Sarah's life. A medical professional would most certainly want to discuss the care of her patient. The cooking and the little extras were just to help James get out of an obvious state of depression. Ironically, James was pretending to be depressed around Willow just to avoid letting her down. James pulled the bowl of stew closer and began shoveling it in his mouth, all the while smiling over at Willow.

"This is really good stew, Willow. You are an excellent cook. I really appreciate it," said James.

"Okay, no flattering my stew just to get off the hook. I need to be convinced you are truly going to be okay alone in this house at night taking care of your ailing wife. There is no shame in telling me it is too much to handle, James."

Finishing up a final bite of stew, James took a piece of bread and mopped up the last bit of gravy then wiped his mouth. James turned in his chair so that he was facing Willow. Their knees were almost touching as took both of her hands in his.

"Willow, this is quite embarrassing, but I thought you were hitting on me in a romantic way, so I started avoiding you by acting down and tired when I arrived home. Now before you tell me how silly that was, please hear me out. I am so sorry. You are not only our nurse, but you are our friend and I should have trusted you."

James paused to take a cleansing breath. "The truth is, I am fine. More than fine, actually. Several months ago, I was swallowed up and lost in my grief, then I had a breakthrough. A group counselor asked me a question that changed my life and my attitude concerning the death of our son Joshua. That night, after I came home from the meeting, yes, I was ready to stop trying, but a miracle occurred. A true amazing, glorious miracle. If you are willing to keep an open mind, I would love to tell you about it. I haven't told anyone before now."

20~Fifth Night

A week had gone by way too fast it seemed after James and Willow had an all revealing conversation. Suddenly everything paled in comparison. The fifth and final meeting of the "Special Good-byes Club" had finally arrived. Quite a bit happened in that week at the Arnold household and he and Willow finally understood each other. Surprisingly, James found Willow very receptive to the story he told of the night he heard the small voice that stopped him from making a bad choice he would have regretted.

James was always nervous as the final night got closer, hoping everything fell into place. It was pizza night, so James called the local joint to put in the order and planned to pick it up on his way to the community center. After hanging up the phone, he jogged upstairs to change his clothes and grab Joshua's favorite stuffed Dinosaur.

"Last night, huh?"

"Yes, and you know I have to take the T-rex remember?"

"I remember."

"Everything always goes smoothly, but I still get nervous…"

"Nah, everything is set, Dad. No worries. Funny group this time, don't ya think?"

"They have given me cause to have a giggle a few times"

"You know I can't go with you, but I will be here when you get back as usual."

"I know."

Turning back for one more time, James asked, "Does it bother you being stuck in this house with me and your mom…I mean if you ever want to leave…"

"I am fine, really. I am okay remember?"

"I remember, I remember everything."

Giving the stuffed dinosaur a quick hug, James lovingly placed it in his duffle bag and zipped it shut. He checked the buttons on his plaid shirt and pulled on his shoelaces to tighten them up. Walking over to give Sarah, he gave her a kiss on the cheek then smoothed her hair before heading downstairs. Before he reached the bottom, he heard Willow using her keys to open the front door. James continued down the stairs, flashing Willow a big grin. She stood at the bottom in her blue hospital scrubs and a wool coat. Her hair was pulled up in a tight bun with wisps of hair framing her face.

"Looks like I got here just in time. All set for the big night?" asked Willow.

"All set. Remember, I might run a little late tonight Willow, but when I return home I will give you a full report"

"I look forward to it James. You packed the dinosaur, right?" asked Willow.

"He is in the bag. Now I am off to pick up pizza."

"Pizza night, huh? Hope all goes well. Are they waiting up stairs for me?" asked Willow smiling as they passed in the foyer.

"Yes, go on up. See you soon" said James as he walked past Willow and out the front door, being sure to close it behind him.

The night air was getting cooler with the setting sun. The full harvest moon was replacing the darkness with a glow that turn the night from darkness to comforting. Native Americans named it the corn moon or harvest moon because it was the time to harvest the corn. A full moon made the fifth night of the meeting extra special. James believed all things were possible under the light of the moon.

After stopping at the local pizza joint on Highway 301, James turned the car toward the community center with nervous anticipation. The smell of pepperoni pizza wafting from the back seat had him salivating. Tonight was a special night and he hoped the parents had followed his instructions and had done their homework.

James arrived juggling the pizza boxes as he switched on the lights, then kicked the door closed with his foot.

Derek and Aaron were standing close to the door when James entered. Seeing the stack of pizza boxes in James's hands, Derek turned and gave Aaron a high five.

"Pizza night! The pattern comes full circle!" shouted Derek.

Aaron returned the high five and shook his head in agreement. "I think we can all agree this dude can hear us and maybe even see us. Or he has some magical powers that allows him to have knowledge of our likes and dislikes."

Five Spirits

Pattimore was sitting in the chair where his mother usually sat; Harry was right next to him. "I am not so sure he can hear us yet, but he may have a spy working for him," said Pattimore.

"What kind of spy?" asked Harry. "Like a 007 kind of spy that drives fast cars and wears sunglasses?"

Aaron and Darcy joined the other two at the circle of chairs while Derek followed James all the way to the refreshment table, keeping a watchful eye on the stack of pizzas.

"I can see the pizza, but I cannot smell it or eat it. I don't think this is fair. The pizza is teasing me!" said Derek as he joined the others, then sat on the floor facing them. "Besides, can't be a spy. We are the only ones here, right?"

Pattimore pushed his glasses up on the bridge of his nose and looked down at Derek. "I don't know if we are alone. We never thought to search the place. Maybe we are not the only ones here."

James stepped back to take a look at the table. Everything had to be perfect for the final night. Next, James straightened the chairs in the circle and placed the tissue boxes on every other chair before he went to his duffle bag and pulled out his son's favorite dinosaur, the Tyrannosaurus Rex. James smiled looking at the stuffed toy in his hands. The short arms and big eyes gave him a giggle. Many times, when Sarah could not reach a dish on the top shelf, they joked she had T-Rex arms. *What amazing joy and fascination this one simple toy has brought to our family*," he thought.

Walking to his usual chair in the circle, he gently placed the stuffed toy facing the room, then walked toward the door to begin greeting parents. Glancing down at his watch, James whispered, "We fear because we forget to hope. Tonight, there is hope"

"This James dude is talking to himself again," said Derek.

"Perhaps he is talking to you, Derek. I have questioned whether or not he can see us; however, that does not mean he can't say things just so we can hear him," Pattimore observed.

"I guess that makes sense. He has given clues almost every night before leaving the building," Derek acknowledged.

Pattimore rose from his position on the floor and began walking around the circle, stopping in front of each spirit. "Of course, it makes sense. It is the only thing that makes any sense right now. The five of us are sitting here: Darcy who died in a crash; Harry who died in the hospital; Aaron was crushed between two boulders Derek who lost his will to face his problems: and then there's me, who blew myself up in the kitchen. We only have one thing in common, don't you see?"

"What are you trying to say? We already know how we died."

Aaron adjusted his seating and began to slowly clap. "Little dude has a point. We would not have met each other had we not died. There has to be a reason we are here and hopefully it was to hear all the outpouring of love from our parents. This James guy must have something big planned for the last night."

"Besides pizza?' laughed Derek. "Nothing is better than pizza."

The five of them started to laugh, then Aaron motioned for one last final group hug. Harry was the first to stand up, followed by Darcy and Pattimore. It was then that the first parents entered the community center. Harry looked up, breaking from the others. "This is it guys, my mom just walked in with Pattimore's mom. Let's go to the back of the room and listen. Whatever happens, happens…"

Harry's mother, Melanie Thomas, came through the doors of the community center with Ruth Gilliam, Pattimore's mother, right behind her. Both ladies were chipper, chatting, and dressed in cotton white dresses with matching shoes. James greeted them, complimenting them on their choice of outfits. Harry's mother stood tall and smoothed out her dress. "We have had a busy week, James. We have been cleaning that old house of mine from top to bottom, got Ruth all moved in and medical equipment gone. So, I decided we deserved a treat. We bought matching dresses for our final night. Fancy, huh?" said Harry's mother, giving a little twirl.

"You ladies look absolutely stunning. However, tonight is pizza night, so I hope you ladies aren't messy eaters!" he laughed.

Next through the door were Mr. and Mrs. Williams, Darcy's parents. James noticed a little bounce in their step and they were holding hands as they walked to their seats. "I can smell the pizza in the air, James," said Nan Williams.

Next, Aaron's parents arrived; right behind them was Derek's mother. All the parents were exchanging nods and asking about their week.

"Smells like pizza in here. Will there still be coffee, James?" asked Mrs. Tenner. "I love my coffee"

"Yes, there will be coffee as well as some water and soft drinks. If you want, help yourself before we get started."

James stood with his legs apart and back straight as he folded his hands in front of him. He always enjoyed the final night of the group meetings. Parents that arrived the first night full of fear, anger and no hope were now conversing with each other like longtime friends. Fearlessly, they were allowing their grief to form a coral reef, hard but brittle, that the algae of hurt grows over. In time, the algae would form into the softest covering. Always there but not forgotten, especially when our loved ones become an empty chair at our table.

As the parents began to find their way to the circle of chairs, James took his usual place in the middle to address them.

"When a person you love becomes a memory, that memory becomes a treasure. This being our final night, we must talk about the fifth stage of grief: acceptance. If we refer back to the first stages, you will see that they all intertwine. At first stage of denial, we cannot imagine ever accepting the death of a child. It is inconceivable. We must all pass through the stages to get here. It is the only way to acceptance. When you move through the anger stage, bargaining, and hit depression, it is like you crawled out of a pit but it was short lived… then you find yourself falling back into a deeper pit of depression. We can't live there. We must try again to reach the final stage."

James moved over to take his seat in the circle, an empty chair on either side. Empty except for his son's stuffed dinosaur. He glanced at the dino and took a cleansing breath before he continued. Crossing one leg over the other he clasped his hands together and laid them in his lap.

"I believe I gave you all some homework. I asked you to answer a question and we will go over the answers tonight. The question was this: *What would it take for you to have acceptance and peace with your child's death?"*

"Who will be brave and read their answer aloud for everyone? I cannot go first for obvious reasons, but does anyone feel up to sharing with us?" asked James.

At first not one parent spoke up. James scanned the room, looking for the signs of hesitation until Derek's mother raised her hand.

"I know exactly what would give me peace. I will go first. Excluding a miracle of course, I would want to talk to my boy one more time and let him know he was loved."

While munching on their pizza most other parents nodded in agreement. James nodded as well. "I think the room agrees with you, Mrs. Tenner"

Mr. and Mrs. Williams, the parents of Darcy, who had gone back for seconds on pizza sat down and gave a sigh. "The Mrs. and I thought about it all week. I don't think anything could make us forget or get over it for longer than an hour. Occasionally, we watch a movie and the pain leaves us but something always reminds us. So, our answer is pretty much the same as Derek's mom…only a miracle, in our opinion."

Slowly going around the room, the parents seemed to tell the scenario the same way with various twists. Convinced nothing really could allow them to accept their loss. Pausing so everyone could enjoy their slice of pizza, James thought of a story his father once told him, so he stood and slowly walked around the circle of chairs.

"I think we can all agree that a pizza has many components. We have the crust, sauce, toppings, and cheese. However, some of those ingredients can stand on their own and some you would never consider anything but an enhancement. I can eat cheese all by itself, but I would not want to consume tomato sauce alone nor would I the crust, perhaps. Another way of looking at it is that the basics are needed as a foundation, but the added toppings can change with each individual's preference. Pizza allows for infinite choices and creativity. We get to decide and make deliberate decisions about what we want, like, or desire. Everyone can decide what would make them happy when ordering a pizza, pineapple or no pineapple. Then we should also be able to decide what would make us feel comfortable in accepting loss. We can try different toppings and we can also try different classes and therapies so that acceptance is the final step we want to achieve."

The room was quiet. Only the humming of the coffee machine could be heard.

As James took his seat again, he leaned forward and spoke softly. "All of us have tried different groups. Look at them as plain cheese pizza. The basics are there but we are not satisfied. We need the pepperoni on top and then add some sausage. That doesn't convince us, either. We want that special thing, that topping that will convince us that this is the best. We need those jalapeño peppers or maybe the side of ranch dressing to dip it in before we vote this the best pizza or the best group session."

As they ate their pizza, the parents quieted down. The five spirits in the room sat close together on the floor and listened intently to how their parents reacted to the pizza analogy. Everyone in the room, living and dead, could sense something different was in the air, something very special.

"I have never thought of pizza the way James described it before now. I have always been a pepperoni guy. Who knew I could have tried different toppings? The world could have been my pizza if I had made better choices," mumbled Derek.

"We all had choices. Every morning you wake up to the sun shining and choices to be made. Is it going to be a good day or a bad day?" replied Darcy.

"Does anyone else get the feeling something is different tonight?" asked Pattimore, crossing his arms. "My mom brought my stuffed horse and I can't stop staring at it."

Harry scooted closer to Pattimore, tucking an arm through his and leaning his head gently on his shoulder. "I feel it, too, but I am not scared. I feel at peace." whispered Harry.

Pattimore gave Harry a slight squeeze then ruffled his dark curly mop of hair. "I don't care if you lick windows or pee on yourself, Harry, you are pretty friggin' special!"

"Thanks, Pattimore. I think you are special, too!"

"It's my big butt and short arms that makes me special, Harry."

"Eww… Gross, you two! Now is not the time for jokes. It is the last night of the group meetings, then we will never see our parents again. I want to soak it all up and remember these five weeks if that is possible.

Five Spirits

We are still unsure what is going to happen to us yet, but like Pattimore, I keep staring at the purple dinosaur my mother brought tonight. I have had that thing since birth. Slept with it every night. Why am I so drawn to it?" said Aaron.

"It is what we are drawn to by our memories, I suppose," replied Darcy. "Something that has touched a part of us now can be held in their hands. Maybe they can sense us when they touch it?"

"James is going to speak again. Let's listen…" whispered Derek as he stood up. "I am feeling a little anxious."

"That is because your mind is drooling over that pizza," laughed Aaron.

As the last of the pizza boxes were discarded, James stood again to address the parents. The mood in the room was morose with everyone understanding this was the last meeting, so James proceeded with caution, knowing how it will all end in just a short while.

"There was a second part to your homework and that was to bring an item that was special to your child. I see all of you understood the assignment," James said, smiling. "I have shown you the T-Rex that belonged to my son, Joshua, and I brought it again tonight. It should be an item that offers something in the way of comfort to your child and you. Why do you think I asked you to do that?"

Immediately raising her hand, Derek's mother sat forward in her chair. "I am sure about this one," she said.

"Please share your thoughts with us, Mrs. Tenner," said James.

Nervously clearing her throat, she pulled a trophy and metal car out of her handbag and held the trophy up before clutching it to her chest and closing her eyes. "This trophy was the first trophy my son, Derek, ever won. He slept with it for the longest time. He set it on the dinner table next to him while he ate. He treasured it. Now it is a fond memory special to him and me. When the person you love becomes a memory, that memory becomes a treasure. Derek was my treasure. Now all I have left is his treasures."

"That is very well said," commented Darcy's mother. "I agree with you. Everything Darcy touched or slept with or cherished is now my treasured memories."

"The toppings on their pizza of life?" chimed in Aaron's father.

Nodding his head, James agreed. "That is one way of looking at it."

One by one, the parents held up and showed the room the precious item that brought joy or comfort to their child. Harry's mother held up a doll made of rags. "Harry couldn't be around plastic or latex so I made him a doll of well-washed linen rags and cotton towels. Some days it was a soldier or a king and some days it was the heroine of a play or his pretend girlfriends," she smiled. "My Harry was special in that he found a way to work around his allergies and make lemonade out of lemons."

Pattimore's mother was the last to share. She picked up the stuffed horse she brought and gave it a quick squeeze. "Holding this simple stuffed horse, I can sense his presence. I feel Pattimore around me and in the room, even now as I hold it in my arms... I feel him near me. I never knew why he loved it so much. All I know is it made him smile. Now that I have moved in with Harry's mother, it has been my comfort and constant companion. I am afraid to wash it and chance losing its smell"

"It's Huckleberry, my stuffed horse!" shouted Pattimore.

Darcy threw an arm around Pattimore and gave him a squeeze. "That is the stuff horse you told us about, Pattimore. It must bring you happiness to see your mom brought it."

James felt himself choking back the tears as he reached for his son's T-Rex and held it in his arms. "Our children left us with little pieces of love. We can never forget them. These seemingly miniscule pieces of memories are the stepping stones that will lead us to acceptance and give us comfort."

Derek's mother nodded her head in agreement. "I had some people tell me I should donate Derek's belongings or sell them at a yard sale. I could never do that."

22~ Acceptance

Harry's mother stood after a few minutes of silence. The only noise in the room was the sound of many tissues being pulled from the boxes. Tears from holding items that belonged to their children sent memories flowing through the room like a wild river. "I took the liberty of baking a carrot cake in honor of our last night together. It should go well with the pizza, so I am just going to put it on the refreshment table if now is a good time?"

Looking very pleased, James stood and announced a break for cake was appropriate. Derek, Aaron, Darcy, Pattimore, and Harry who had been huddled together mesmerized by all the tokens brought by their parents, leaned back, then formed a circle facing each other.

"I guess it is true that we can't take anything with us but we can leave something behind," commented Aaron. "Pieces of love, as James so aptly put it."

"It was beautiful. I remember the first night when we watched our parents come in. This is different. My mother was not crying like she did the first night. She seemed content somehow holding my stuffed horse," said Pattimore as he stared at the others.

"They are surviving, pulling it together, maybe they are going to be okay," said Derek. "Do any of you feel that way?"

"My mother made a cake. She hasn't baked a cake since I can remember. She is different – like she changed somehow," Harry said as he picked at the rubber on his shoes. "I notice a change."

Darcy leaned in toward the others. "Listen, we wanted them to be okay, to continue to live and thrive. I saw my mother smile when Pattimore's mother shared his stuffed horse and when she pulled my old doll and karaoke microphone out of her purse, my dad actually let out a chuckle. This is what we wanted. Somehow, we did it. It happened and they are going to live on and never forget us."

"I agree. Our parents will always have our little pieces of love to remember us by," boasted Aaron. "What comes next for us, I wonder?"

"If this is them having acceptance, then I guess that means our parents will be okay and hopefully there will be nothing to keep us here, I suppose," replied Darcy.

As the parents were busy delighting in the luxurious carrot cake, James walked around casually chatting, then ended up very close to the spirits sitting on the floor. "It won't be long now" he whispered. Then, just as casually, he returned to the snack table surrounded by smiling parents.

Slowly the parents meandered around, ending up back in their seats. There was no more idle chatter but more of a feeling of hesitation, lacking confidence. James waited for each to take their seats before he again stood and paced around the circle preparing to present the final part of the group session. This part was always a bag of mixed emotions both for the parents and for James. Getting to know the parents in such an intimate way then saying good bye to prepare for the next was emotionally hard but made him confident that his unique methods were needed by so many.

Clearing his throat, James stood with his arms folded. "I asked a hard question of you and received many answers. As I explained to you all before, I was asked this same question by a concerned counselor. When I felt I discovered the best possible answer, it changed my life. So now I am going to tell you what the best answer is and hopefully it will change you life as well."

James paused and looked down for a brief moment, trying hard to maintain his composure. Looking up again he continued. "I asked what it would take for you to accept your child's death. Not forget, but accept. There is a difference. After long thought and a few impossible answers, I came up with this while thinking about my son, Joshua. As a father, I consider the pain factor, the fear, and the loneliness I held on to when my mind wandered to the death of Joshua. Did he feel pain or fear without me being by his side?"

Looking around the silent room at each parent's face, he got the feeling they were thinking the same things as most parents do. "So, I decided whole heartedly that if I could know without any doubt that my son was going to be okay. No pain, sorrow or fear… just peace. I and his mother could release some of our worry and fear and accept that he is gone. It is not by any means what we wanted but it happened. Joshua died. If he has gone on to heaven with peace, then I must accept it and live with my memories of the time we had that were full of love. Basically, my answer is this, If I know my child is free with no worldly pain or worries then I can be okay and live on. Does everyone understand what I am saying?"

Darcy's mother was the first to react. Leaning forward and placing her hands over her face, she took a deep breath before she looked up. "I have been in agony wondering if my daughter, Darcy, felt any pain. It has been my worst fear. If I knew she was made whole again after death that would take a big weight off my shoulders. How is that possible to know?"

"We are just supposed to have faith that my Harry is jumping and swinging from the chandelier with out even a wheeze? I always thought I had that kind of faith but at times all I can think is 'is he okay?'" asked Ms. Thomas. "When it is 3:00 p.m., I still startle thinking it is medication time for Harry, then I remember he is not here. Is someone giving his medication?"

James held his hands up, stopping the conversation for a moment. He did not want the worry to appear back in the faces of the parents like was on the first night.

"Let's hold on a minute. I am saying *IF* you knew for sure the children were fine, would that give you relief? If by faith or by proof, it would certainly give you the power to accept they are gone. Ms.

Thomas, If you knew Harry could run and turn cartwheels without losing his breath or that Aaron was standing tall and not struggling to breathe from being crushed, Darcy was not in pain from the accident or if Pattimore's face was restored. Would you be at ease enough to let them go, cherish their pieces of love they left behind and live on?"

Tears spilled as each parent contemplated the idea of their child no longer suffering any defects, no pain, and no deformities. That they were made whole and transformed after death. James began seeing the nods as the possibilities filled their minds. He did not wait for a response before he continued. James glanced over at the spirits huddled in a circle clinging to each other while listening to his every word and shot them a quick wink.

Looking back at the parents, he continued. "At the same time, is it possible that your children also have the same thoughts about you as well? Perhaps they could be in your presence, maybe listening to you or watching you as you grieve. They also want to know that you as the parent are going to be okay without them. We have all told stories of feeling our child's presence, especially when clinging to one of the items they used to cherish. With faith or proof, we have to consider that they want to also be sure you are going to live on before they leave us. Children bring us great joy in life. When that joy is removed, is it possible to continue without it? It can leave a giant hole in our lives."

Derek's mother, Mrs. Tenner, grabbed a tissue to wipe her eyes then straightened her back before taking a sip of her coffee. "I would like to know. I believe in heaven, raised in the church. I would love to know and believe that my Derek is playing baseball and driving race cars in heaven with his father, who has also passed on. There is no confirmation even if you believe or have faith. That is the hard part. I can have faith and hope it to be true. However sometimes that is not enough. I want to *know* and I want to *see* the proof for myself but I don't think that is possible."

James took a step closer to the group and looked hard into their eyes. "That is the ultimate problem facing everyone who has lost a child or any loved one when it comes to the final stage of acceptance: 'How can I be sure my child is okay and again, how can they know I am okay?' If faith is enough, then you reach the final stage. However, for those of us who question everything or have no faith, we struggle to reach acceptance. That is why I created this special group."

Aaron's father grunted loudly expressing his doubt. "So, if we just have some kind of magic faith, we are okay? That is it? That is what you are saying?"

"I am saying that is one way or there is another way…"

23~ Ethereal

"Ethereal" can refer to anything heavenly or airy, specifically to regions beyond earth not usually seen in common day to day life, or belief. Extremely delicate and light in a way that is sometimes too perfect.

James sat, legs crossed and arms folded in his chair at the circle, allowing time for questions and comments. He recalled in his mind how on his drive to the center tonight, he took notice of the show the stars were putting on in the sky. A curtain of deep blue velvet thick with the shimmering of various stars complimenting the full harvest moon. It was setting up to be a perfect night. *"All things are possible under the light of the moon,"* he thought to himself. He quietly observed as the parents discussed their doubts, beliefs and exchanged their feelings on having faith. Listening and watching as he did every last day of his five week sessions giving time for all the parents grasping to comprehend what had occurred in the last five weeks. He also gave in to several glances at the five huddled spirits watching his every move with hopeful apprehension. Anticipation was building as parents questioned everything until it was time to accept anything. They were eager to know more while dissecting the previous words of James concerning faith and proof.

Standing, James clasped his hands in front of him and bowed his head as he searched for the right words. It wass not always the same speech of words, every group of parents were different. When he cleared his throat, he scanned the room with his eyes hoping to catch the attention of every adult and spirit in the room while at the same time being reticent about his own thoughts. He was setting the stage, preparing for what lies ahead.

When the mood was just right and he could feel their hearts beating in their chests, he lifted his head and began the final words to end the special good bye group.

"There is something worse than grief and that is feeling nothing. We let grief come and stay as long as it needs to. We let it go and we let it come back again. Grief will never end as long as you love the one who is gone. Sometimes your grief will feel like the clouds in the sky hovering over you, suffocating. Some days it is a laugh that feels really good. Grief and memories are formless, they come and go like the tide on the beach. Your scars of healing from loss will itch longer and more inconsistently than any wound you have ever experienced."

James continued, "Notice the empty chairs beside you in the room. Our loved ones have become the empty chair, their favorite song on the radio, the touch of their skin or the smell of their freshly washed hair. Grief is not the enemy. It is now part of your normal and when it hits you, wrap up in it like warm blanket until it passes. It is not gone forever, it will return in the form of unexpected memories."

As the words sank in, James observed parents clutching tightly to the special item belonging to their child as they stared at the empty chairs next to them as though it was the first time they noticed.

The only sound was the swoosh of wiping tears. Mrs. Tenner slowly rested her free hand on the empty chair beside her and closed her eyes. James nodded to the spirits and motioned for them to walk toward their parents. One by one, as they became aware of James's request, they took a seat in the empty chairs next to their respective parents. Pattimore winked and James returned the gesture confirming what the spirits suspected all along: James could indeed hear them and see them. Darcy smiled at James, feeling calm about the awareness as though he was an old family friend here to help. There was no hint of fear. The words James softly spoke placed peace and mutual trust in the air as parents and spirit coexisted.

A short, quiet pause fell over the group as James was privy to the perfect full circle that no longer had empty chairs. Smiling, James slowly took a few steps back and took his seat, then turned his eyes on the empty chair next to him. Joshua's favorite stuffed dinosaur perched proudly staring back at him.

"It is time," James said softly. "There is a giant full moon giving off the softest violet hue tonight. Hold tightly to the items you brought that gave great comfort to your child and let us walk out into the evening and look toward the moon. All of us."

Five Spirits

James met with the eyes of the five spirits, letting them know that they, too, were leaving the community center to gaze at the moon.

Derek was the first to stand. "We can leave?" he whispered.

"All of us. It is the right time," said James.

Pattimore looked over at Harry and, grabbing his hand, the two of them walked out together following their parents. Aaron and Derek, being the gentlemanly type, stood one on each side of Darcy to escort her out in style. Darcy chuckled, lifting her chin. She circled her arm in each of theirs and the three of them strutted through the door being the last of the spirits to leave followed by James.

The parents formed a line of sorts, facing the breathtaking full moon. James took his place behind the parents forming a line with the spirits. The spirits were feeling giddy just being outside of the stuffy community center.

James waited an appropriate amount of time for the moon to work its magic with its radiance showing on the faces of the group. It was time to reflect and appreciate the lives left behind. James looked back and forth at the spirits having a hard time standing still while trying to contain the feeling of being free and whole.

"I want to run, run through the field, and jump into that moon like a pool of water," said Harry, wiggling his legs.

"Am I the only one that is feeling drawn toward the sky? It is like the stars are calling my name and lifting my feet off the ground," whispered Darcy.

Brushing his hair back with both hands, keeping them on top of his head as he twisted his body back and forth, Aaron chimed in. "I feel light as a feather, like a weight has been lifted. What is happening?"

"I think I can fly," whispered Derek.

Staring straight ahead, James squeezed Joshua's beloved dinosaur. Looking up into the stars sparkling in the night sky, his eyes started to burn with tears.

"Then you must go… You are free spirits. You must move on"

In one lightning-swift move, the five spirits who were standing behind their parents were pulled by an unknown source, passing swiftly through the physical body of their parents and creating a rush of wind. Looking back occasionally as they ran toward the meadow, they jumped, waved, and skipped gleefully. The velvet curtain thick with stars seemed to part like the drapes at a theater on Broadway as the five spirits of Darcy, Derek, Pattimore, Aaron and Harry drifted into the shadow of the moon.

Just as their silhouettes dancing free and whole was the only thing left to be seen, little Harry turned back and gave a wave to his mother. A signal to let her know he was once again a healthy whole boy, able to breathe and play.

They were gone, leaving only the image of the vast majestic moon. Completely shocked and disbelieving the parents stood frozen, afraid to move, hoping that if they stood perfectly still the sight they just experienced would not go away like a magician's card trick. Turning to look at James with her mouth gaping, Darcy's mother broke down in tears. One by one, they turned with dumbfounded looks on their faces as though begging for confirmation to the miracle they just encountered.

"I asked you if you could be sure your children were not in pain, made whole again and at peace would you be able to live on? You have bonded with other parents by this experience. A special good-bye that you will never forget but will be unable to explain. Now can you freely live on in acceptance holding on to what you just saw, never forgetting your children are free? They spent their whole life with you. You, as parents, need to live on and your loved ones need to move on."

"I saw him. It was my Pattimore. I know it was. He is perfect now," cried Mrs. Gilliam. "I saw him turn and wave good-bye!"

There was a different sparkle in their eyes, mixed with the tears, almost glowing. Not a word was spoken as the parents slowly shuffled back toward the community center to gather their belongings. Darcy's parents grabbed James for a group hug before they walked out the door, too emotional to speak. Harry's mother took the hand of Ruth, the mother of Pattimore, sharing a smile they left the center in their matching dresses, giving a silent nod toward the other parents. Mr. and Mrs. Jackson, the parents of Aaron, were next to leave giving a slight wave then quickly bowing their heads as they hurried out. Derek's mother was the last to leave, hanging back to speak to James.

"Is everything alright, Mrs. Tenner?"

"It is hard to find words right now James. I was always afraid the confirmation that my boy, Derek, was going to be okay would never come. I will not ask you how you made it happen, I just want to say thank you… Thank you for my special good-bye. It gave me comfort. I saw him run. I saw him smiling that beautiful smile of his. I know now that my Derek is where he is supposed to be."

"Have a good night, Mrs. Tenner"

As she reached the door, Mrs. Tenner turned back one last time. "Have they been here the whole time listening to us?"

"Yes."

"Then my Derek knows how much I love him?"

Five Spirits

"He knows."

When Derek's mother left, James closed the door and took a deep breath before starting his clean up routine. He tossed the pizza boxes and cleaned the coffee pot. Noticing there was one piece of the carrot cake left that Harry's mother brought, he decided to wrap it up to take home to Willow. After all, she has been a great support even after James explained the details of the secret group.

James drove straight home instead of driving around to kill time. Willow would be waiting, and he no longer needed to avoid her as he did in the past.

Pulling into the driveway, grabbing the piece of cake he had delicately placed next to him on the front seat, he began to briskly walk up the sidewalk to the front door. The weather was beginning to turn cold early this fall and he had failed to bring a jacket.

"I take it everything went well tonight according to the look on your face, James," said Willow.

"Yes, it was a fine send-off. I wish you could have seen it, Willow."

"Perhaps I will someday. Dinner is ready if you haven't filled up on pizza," she chuckled.

"No, I am starving. I never eat during the meetings. I can't take a chance that I will be talking and a piece of pepperoni is stuck in my teeth. I brought you some carrot cake."

Willow took the cake, smiled, then turned toward the kitchen as James stared upstairs. "I think I will just pop up and say hello. I will be down in a minute."

Upstairs, James entered the room where his wife, Sarah, laid quietly. Near the pillow, stroking his mother's hair, was Joshua smiling at seeing his father enter the room.

"It was a good night, I suppose, the full moon and all. I assume everyone was happy and amazed?" Joshua smiled his toothy grin. *"I took the liberty of selecting the next group for you and already made contact,"* said Joshua. *"This next group is a bit less timid than the previous one, and talkative too. Sadly ,one was a victim of a school shooting."*

"Thank you, Joshua, a rowdy bunch, huh?"

"How ever they were in life is how they stay after death personality wise. You just got lucky with me, I was nice and oh a very cool dude. More girls this time. Remember when you told me girls had cooties?"

"I will look over the files and send the invitation letters out tomorrow, I trust your judgment, Joshua. New group starts next week. And yes, you were a very cool dude"

"I heard you say it was getting cold. Will it snow? I miss the snow"

"It is too early for snow. Did I ever tell you it was snowing when I met your mother? A faint snow of fluffy flakes as I walked her to her dorm room. Young and bold we danced on her front stoop, neither of us wanting to say good-bye. We could have caught a cold or worse, but I loved that night. Your mother was beautiful covered in snow flakes"

Looking over at his wife, Sarah, he noticed a peaceful look on her face. Her skin was like porcelain, James leaned in for a kiss. "Her lips are warm. Does she have a fever?"

"I think she does. I cannot feel it, but I heard Willow on the phone with the doctor. If Mom…umm… leaves us, will it be okay if I go with her so she won't be alone?'

James again felt the burning in his eyes. "I wish I could hug you right now. You have not only helped me, but hundreds of grieving parents. I would have to stop the secret good-bye club without you to help. Your mom will not be alone. Millions have gone before her and will be waiting to greet her as she moves on"

Feeling selfish, James turned to focus on the hazy figure of his son. "I cannot stop you, Joshua. If you must go, I will live on."

"Probably not until after this next meeting at least. It's just that I know you are going to be okay now, Dad. You have Willow."

"Willow has helped, but you know I am so proud of you, Son. Together, we have helped hundreds of people with their stages of grief. I'd better go down and eat dinner. Don't want to eat a cold dinner. Seriously, don't stay just for me. I will be fine."

James quickly turned away, hoping Joshua did not see the trail of tears beginning to flow. Rushing downstairs, James only paused once to lean against the wall and wipe the tears from his cheeks.

During dinner ,Willow and James shared idle talk as James thumbed through the files for the next group. Half listening, James took out his small notebook and began writing details about each parent and child that was to be invited to the next five week sessions.

"James, did you hear what I said? I think it is time I moved into the house. My lease is up next month, and I want to be here for you when the time comes. What do you think about it?"

"Think about what?"

"Oh, James! Me moving in, I want to know what you think."

"Whatever you decide, Willow, is fine with me."

"That was not reassuring, but I know you are busy. We can talk about it when I come tomorrow. Put your plate in the sink for me, okay? I need to get home and start packing."

"Good night, Willow."

*　　*　　*　　*　　*

When you are focused on any good cause, time seems to fly by in the blink of an eye. Sarah became weaker and her breathing more shallow each day. When James was not by her side, he was planning for the next five-week session. James sent out the invitations for the next group and all five families responded. The night finally came for the first meeting and James was hesitant to leave the house.

"Go ahead, Dad, I will be here, and Mom will be okay."

James nodded, closing the door quietly. James drove to the Riverview Community Center early enough to start the coffee and prepare the snack table as he did and would do every night during the five weeks. After it was all set with a bright fuchsia table cloth, he carefully displayed a plate of assorted french macaroons of every color. When he next started putting the chairs in a circle, leaving one empty chair between, he heard a delicate, otherworldly voice coming from the corner of the room.

"What is happening? Why am I here?"

James continued placing boxes of tissues on every other chair, trying not to acknowledge what he was hearing. Still, a barely perceptible smile found its way to his lips.

"Look! My absolute favorite snack. Can this dude hear us or something? I swear I saw him trying to hide a smile."

"How did we get here? Last thing I remember is going on a rope swing over the Alafia River."

"How many of us are here?"

*"*I *count five of us. Five spirits in the room!"*

As James turned away, he smiled warmly, knowing that the five weeks ahead would be incredible.

About the Author

Rebecca is a writer of Historical Fiction and fantasy novels. She retired from hospital work after 27 years, and now lives with her husband in Florida. She loves including historical facts, cities, and sites in her books alongside fictional characters. It is her passion to include strong female heroines in her books as well.

Her three grown children and three grandchildren keep her busy, but never too busy to write full time.

Rebecca spent her early childhood in Texas before moving to Florida. She enjoys writing and including stories about the places she has lived or visited in her books.

Five Spirits

End Notes, disclaimers, etc...

All the characters in my books are fictional. I hope you enjoy <u>Five Spirits in the Room</u> as much as I did writing it. I enjoy including strong female lead characters in my novels and "Angel Moms" are some of the strongest women I know. You may also enjoy some of my other novels and lastly, teach your children to read...

Mother always told me: *"If you can read, you can do anything..."*

Sincerely,

Rebecca Conaty Bruce

Five Spirits

ACKNOWLEDGEMENTS

Thank you to Amy @ prettysleepyart.net for her art work used on the cover of several of my books, including this one.

Thank you to Author Michael Paul Hurd, owner of Lineage Independent Publishing, who was always there encouraging me to keep writing and suggesting edits. Thank you for sharing your knowledge with me.

Thank you to my family who never stopped believing in me.

Thank you to my mother in heaven. I did it mom!

Five Spirits

The Irish Bones Series – A two book Historical Fiction series following Lovina, whose father on his death bed tells her she has Irish Bones. Lovina reflects back on how she discovered her Irish Bones through the stories of her Irish Granddad. Book I captures you in the struggles of the past, Book II is her life after leaving Ireland. Rated for 18 and up.

Follow Me

Facebook: Facebook.com/Irishbonesbook1

Twitter: @Rebecca29971384

Website: https://rebeccaconatybruceauthor.com/

Instagram: Rebecca.a.bruce

Email: Irishbones310@gmail.com

Rebecca Conaty Bruce is also featured on Lineage Independent Publishing's web page, https://lineage-indypub.com